Amy Cross is the author of more than 200 horror, paranormal, fantasy and thriller novels.

OTHER TITLES
BY AMY CROSS INCLUDE

THE
DEVIL
ON
DAVIS
DRIVE

MERCY WILLOW BOOK NINE

AMY CROSS

CONTENTS

THE
DEVIL
ON
DAVIS
DRIVE

PROLOGUE

Twenty years earlier...

"HELLO, MERCY WILLOW. HOW are you today?"

Sitting in the same chair I've sat in so many times before, I stare at Doctor Ross and find myself wondering exactly what he wants me to say. I've long since come to the conclusion that these meetings are completely pointless, and I feel as if we're going round and round in circles. Sometimes he talks to me when I'm Mercy, sometimes he talks to me when I'm Jessica, and sometimes he talks to me when I'm Annabelle; at the end of the day, however, I really don't think that he's making any progress at all.

"Are you not going to answer?" he asks.

"I don't know what to say."

"Just say whatever comes into your head."

I swallow hard.

"Do you find it hard to differentiate between the thoughts of these three different minds?" he asks as he leans back in his chair, which once again creaks loudly beneath his weight. "Do you have separate thoughts, or is it more the case that you share them with the others?"

"They're mine," I tell him, before pausing. "I think so, anyway."

"But you're not sure?"

"No, I'm sure," I lie. "They're separate thoughts."

"And can you control when and how the different aspects of your personality take over?"

"I think so."

"You only *think* so?"

"Can I be excused, please?" I ask, as I feel the first creeping flicker of an oncoming headache. "I'd like to go back to my room."

"Why's that?" he asks quickly, almost as if he'd been expecting my response and had his counterpoint all lined up. "Does this conversation make you feel uncomfortable, Mercy? Are you perhaps struggling to reconcile the three parts of your personality?"

"No!" I snap back, perhaps a little too hastily.

Sure enough, he makes a note.

"What are you writing down?" I ask.

"It's really nothing."

"I want you to tell me."

"Is this still Mercy I'm talking to?" he replies. "You seem agitated, and I'm used to Mercy being the calmer of the three personalities. Is this maybe some kind of... evolution?"

I open my mouth to reply, and then I hesitate for a few seconds. I always hate it when Doctor Ross comes up with all these silly theories, and I hate playing into his hands. I adjust my position in the chair again, causing it to creak more loudly than ever beneath my weight, and then I sit up a little straighter.

"I'm Mercy," I say calmly, "and I don't rise to the bait. Not the way Jessica or Annabelle might. I'd much prefer to have a pleasant conversation, but if that's not possible today, I'd really rather go back to my room. I'm sorry, Doctor Ross, but I'm not feeling up to very much today and I'd like to find some time to just get my thoughts together. You can understand that, can't you?"

"I understand that you're growing up," he

replies, "and that this must be a very confusing time for you. We're going to have to think about how best to handle things as you stop being a little girl and start becoming a woman. For example, it's quite natural for you to want to rebel and if -"

"I don't want to rebel," I tell him, although in that moment I realize that I'm lying. I feel a faint twitch on one side of my face, although I'm not sure whether that's something that Doctor Ross would necessarily have noticed. "I'm quite happy here. I think it's the best place for me. Really, I can't imagine how I'd cope in the outside world."

***

Later, once I've finally been left alone, I sit on my bed and stare at my reflection in the window. Night is falling outside, and I can see my own face staring back at me. At the same time, I know that behind those eyes there are three distinct personalities, and they're still jostling for control.

"You've taken over too much," I hear Annabelle's voice saying. "It was never meant to be like this. You're just my imaginary friend, that's all."

"You're a murderer," I whisper out loud.

"You didn't stop me."

"I tried."

"She has a point," Jessica's voice adds, and she sounds amused by the situation. "Actually, I'm not sure which of you that was addressed to. I guess both of you idiots need to see some sense."

"You're not helping," I tell her.

"I don't think anyone *can* help," she replies. "We're basically sitting here talking to ourselves. You've got to admit, this whole situation is pretty crazy."

"It's best if I stay in control," I say firmly, hoping that they'll both listen to me. "I'm -"

"You're the squeaky clean perfect Mercy Willow," Annabelle sneers. "You think you're better than both of us."

"I didn't say that."

"But you think it."

I open my mouth to reply to her, but at the last second I hold back. After all, she's right, I *do* think that in some ways I'm the better personality; I'm certainly the one that causes the least trouble, and that leads to the least friction with the outside world. Annabelle's a murderer and Jessica enjoys causing trouble, so that leaves me as the acceptable public face of our little trinity. If the others don't want me to be in control, then I might have to try to find a way to force the issue.

"What are you plotting?" Jessica asks, and

suddenly she sounds worried. "I can usually read your thoughts, but you've found some way to hide them from me, haven't you?"

"Not on purpose," I reply, genuinely surprised by this news.

"Stop it," she continues. "I don't like it."

"Yeah, stop it," Annabelle says. "You have no right to keep any of your thoughts to yourself. Not in our shared head."

Ignoring them both, I continue to stare at our reflection. I know that the other two are annoyed, but I'm starting to think that I really need to come up with a plan. Actually, I already have a plan; what I need is to find a way to put it into action, and for that I'm going to need a little help.

"Jessica?" I say cautiously.

"What?" she snaps.

"Annabelle can't hear us right now," I continue, still watching the window. "I've got an idea, and I need your help. It's the best thing for all three of us, but you're going to think I'm nuts when I explain it."

"I *already* think you're nuts."

"I think you'll like the overall aim, though," I add, hoping against hope that I can get her on my side against Annabelle. "This place is no good for us. It's time for us to get out of the hospital."

CHAPTER ONE

Today...

"YOU KNOW," DOUG BARRYMORE says as we stand outside the house on Davis Drive and watch two men carrying a sofa into the back of a van, "I probably shouldn't admit this, but there were times when I genuinely didn't think we'd ever get the place sold."

"You had a lot of bad luck," I reply, which is something of an understatement. "Everything's sorted now, though. I hope thc move is everything you've been waiting for and more."

"We've loved living in Candleward," he explains, as I see his wife Misha and their daughter Prudence emerging from the house, "but sometimes you've gotta go where the job takes you. In this case, I was made an offer that's too good to refuse. Besides, ten years in Cornwall feels like enough."

Before I can answer, I realize that Prudence is snapping at her mother. I glance at them as they make their way over to join us, and I see that Prudence – who from the very start has struck me as a strange girl – appears to be sulking massively. She briefly makes eye contact with me, and I see the same angry intransigence that I encountered whenever I tried to go near her bedroom. I know teens can be angry, but Prudence seems to take rebellion to a whole new level.

"Got everything?" Doug asks them.

"I can't believe you're *actually* going through with this," Prudence complains. "I don't want to move!"

"We've been through this," Misha replies, turning to her. "Your father's promotion -"

"I don't give a damn about any promotion!" Prudence snaps, before turning and looking back at the house. "I like living here. I don't want to leave it behind and you can't make me!"

"Actually, I think you'll find that we can," Doug says, putting an arm around her shoulder and guiding her past the van, leading her toward their car. "Until you're a little older, you pretty much have to do whatever we tell you. I know that must feel horrible, but it's just the way the world works."

"This is your fault!" Prudence snaps, looking over her shoulder and staring at me. "You've got no idea what you've done!"

"Don't be rude," Misha counsels her.

"None of you know!" Prudence hisses, before pulling the door open and climbing into the car. "I'll never forgive any of you! You're all just idiots!"

"Typical teen angst," Doug says as he turns to me. "Ignore her, Ms. Willow. I can assure you that Misha and I are extremely grateful to you for everything you've done. You really went above and beyond the call of duty. How many times did the chain break down? Six?"

"I've got to admit," I reply, "that's a record for me. But everything's sorted now, and that's what matters." I check my watch. "The Hoopers should be here soon, and then number three Davis Drive will enter a whole new phase."

"It's been a lovely home for us over the years," Misha says, and she seems a little misty-eyed as she turns and looks back at the property. "We'll miss it, but we're also excited about what the future holds." She looks at her husband and, after a moment, pats him on the chest. "Shall we get going? It's a long drive north and I'd really like to get to the new place before it gets dark."

I watch as they climb into the car, and I'm starting to feel that familiar sense of a job well done, the same sense that I get every time a house changes hands. Despite the fact that I might sound corny, I genuinely enjoy helping people get their dream moves. As the Barrymores' car starts to pull away, however, I spot Prudence glaring out at me and I'm reminded that not everyone likes change. Still, I tell myself that she'll get used to the new house eventually and – as their car disappears around the corner – I take a deep breath followed by a sigh as I realize that finally my most troublesome property has been sold.

"You were a tough nut to crack," I mutter, turning to look at the house again. "I was starting to wonder whether this sale was *ever* going to go through."

***

Once I'm back in the house, standing all alone in the empty front room, I realize that there's really no point going back to the office when the new family should arrive within the next hour. I have the keys, so I might as well stick around here and try to amuse myself.

Of course, since there's absolutely no furniture, I have to slide open the back door and step out onto the sun-drenched patio, which to be fair isn't exactly the worst place to wait. I lean against the wall and take my phone out, and I find that I have a couple of messages from Nathan; he's taken to sending me funny videos, usually about two or three a day, and sometimes I even manage to find one to send back to him. I watch these latest videos and I can't help smiling, and after a moment I start searching for something that I might be able to sent to him in return.

And then, with no warning, I hear an almighty crashing sound coming from somewhere upstairs in the house.

Startled, I step back inside and listen, but now silence has returned. There can be no doubt about the sound, however; I definitely heard something heavy smashing around, and it didn't seem to be just one impact. Instead, I'm sure I heard a person bumping around in one of the rooms up there, so after a moment I make my way to the hall and look up the stairs.

"Hello?" I call out, even though I'm pretty sure that there's no-one else here.

I wait, but no-one replies and I'm starting to

try to figure out what else might have caused that commotion. I guess it's possible that the Barrymores left something behind that eventually toppled over, so I start making my way up. After all, I'd hate for the Hoopers to find some kind of damage on their first day here.

"I hope there won't be any silly games," I continue. "There's really no need for that sort of thing, is there? The Barrymores never mentioned anything about a ghost, so obviously you didn't cause too much trouble for them. How about you try to show the Hoopers the same courtesy?"

Reaching the door to the master bedroom, I look through and spot nothing untoward. After just a couple of seconds, however, I hear a scratching sound coming from one of the other rooms and I look over my shoulder. The sound seems to be emanating from Prudence's old bedroom, and in that moment I think back to the way she refused to let me go in there. As a shiver runs up my spine, I start to wonder whether this might be another Candleward house that contains a lingering spirit from long ago. I'm always on the lookout for ghosts, but until this moment the house on Davis Drive hadn't presented with anything obvious.

"Hello?" I say again. "My name's Mercy, you might have seen me before. I'm an estate agent and a new family's about to move in. There's no need to be scared."

I step across the landing and look into the room that used to belong to Prudence. There's no sign of anyone, although I quickly spot the built-in wardrobe at the far end of the room. The last thing I want to do is feed my paranoia, but I walk over and pull the doors open, and to my relief I find nothing in the wardrobe except a bare railing and a few left-over clothes hangers. I guess a ghost might have been hiding earlier, but there's certainly nothing in here now. That doesn't mean, however, that some kind of presence might not be lurking close enough to hear me.

"They seem really nice," I continue, stepping away from the wardrobe and heading back out onto the landing. "There's Matt Hooper, his wife Diane and their two kids. I can't remember the kids' names off the top of my head, but I don't think you've got anything to worry about."

I wait.

Silence.

"Something tells me you're going to be just fine," I add, before looking out the window as I realize I can hear a car on the gravel. Sure enough, a car is pulling up outside and I realize that the Hoopers are here. "This is them," I explain.

"Something tells me that once you get to know them, you're really going to love them. So there's no need to do any mean haunting, okay?"

I wait.

No reply.

"Okay," I add, before adjusting my jacket and then starting to make my way downstairs. "Time to welcome the Hoopers to their new home."

CHAPTER TWO

TWO WEEKS LATER, SITTING at my desk with my phone against the side of my face, I open my mouth and try to speak – only for Frank Chipson to continue without giving me a chance.

"I'd just like your opinion," he says firmly. "Ms. Willow, I've been trying to get you to come out to Gower Grange for a while now and you just seem to keep making excuses. Can't you find five minutes?"

"I really don't understand what it is that you think I can help with," I say cautiously, and that just about sums up the way I've been feeling for a while now. "Mr. Chipson, the sale went through quite a while ago now. The house belongs to you. Unless you've suddenly changed your mind and you want to put it back on the market, the last thing you need is an estate agent."

"I just think there are certain... issues that you could help with."

"Such as?"

I wait, but now he's fallen silent. I've spoken to Frank a few times over the past few weeks, yet somehow he never quite seems able to come out and tell me exactly what's wrong.

"I can't explain over the phone," he says finally. "You need to come and see it for yourself."

"Is that her?" I hear a voice asking, and I realize that Frank's wife must have been listening in to our call the whole time. "Tell her what's going on, Frank!"

"Will you please just leave it to me?" he hisses.

"Listen," I say, keen to get the call over, "how about I drop by one evening after work? I guess I can spare a few minutes."

"Tonight?"

"Not tonight," I tell her. "Can we say... Friday?"

"Is there no way you can come any earlier?"

"I would if I could," I reply, before turning as I see that the door to the office is opening. To my surprise Matt Hooper is making his way inside; I nod at him before trying to think of some way to end the call faster. "I'll drop by on Friday around half past five, Mr. Chipson. That's really the best I can do. It was nice to hear from you, though. Thanks for calling. Goodbye!"

Before he has a chance to answer, I cut the call and set my phone down. I know I might have seemed a little rude just now, but as I turn to Matt I remind myself that I'm far too busy to go running around on wild goose chases.

"Mr. Hooper," I say with a smile, "how are things going in your new home?"

"Great," he replies, although I can immediately tell that he's troubled by something. "Couldn't be better."

"That's wonderful," I tell him. "To be honest, I knew from the outset that the place needed a family. I hope your children are enjoying having such a large garden?"

"It's a great space," he admits. "Katie in particular spends all her time out there. She's taking to Cornish life like a duck to water."

"And your son?"

"Lance is..."

His voice trails off, and I'm fairly sure that we're getting to the crux of the problem.

"Ms. Willow," he continues cautiously, "I

know this is going to sound really strange, and I can't quite believe that I'm about to ask you something so crazy, but my wife thinks it might be good to just... make sure. I'm not for one second accusing anyone of anything, but I just need to know whether that house... our new house... has any history of...”

I wait for him to finish.

“Death,” he adds finally. “Murder.”

He pauses.

“Ghosts,” he mutters, before shaking his head. “There. I said it.”

He sighs and heads to the door.

“Forget it,” he adds, clearly embarrassed. “I'm sorry, can you just pretend that I never came here today?”

“Wait!” I call out, hurrying after him. “Mr. Hooper, is something happening in your new home?”

He turns to me, and I can already see the sense of desperation in his eyes. He's quite clearly clutching at straws, and I can only assume that coming here must have required some real bravery. Sure, I've seen plenty of ghosts since I arrived in Candleward, but I still remember how I felt when I encountered the first one back at Hurst House – and how I worried that I was losing my mind, and that no-one would ever take me seriously. Matt Hooper seems like a level-headed guy and things must be bad if he's come to me now.

"I don't know what's happening," he tells me finally. "I just... can't get it straight in my head."

"Do you want to come in and sit down?" I ask, gesturing toward my desk. "My boss is out right now, and I promise you can tell me anything. I won't judge you."

***

"It's not even as we've actually *seen* anything," he continues a few minutes later, as we sit at the desk and I listen to his story. "It's more of a kind of presence that gets stronger and stronger each day."

"And this presence -"

"I just want to know if the house has any kind of history," he adds, interrupting me. "I did some searching online and I couldn't find anything, but my wife's convinced that there has to be something we're missing. Isn't there some kind of law that states you're required to tell us about anything like that before we buy?"

"That's in America, I think," I tell him, "but obviously I'd have felt morally obliged to inform you if I was aware of something significant."

Although I know that the Barrymores never mentioned anything unusual, I still get to my feet and head over to the filing cabinet. I want Matt to know that I'm taking him seriously, and I also need to play for time. After all, I did notice a few unusual things at the house on Davis Drive, even if at the time I wasn't too worried. If I told potential buyers about *every* hint of ghostly activity I detected, I'd never get a single house sold, so I've developed a tendency to only worry if something seems dangerous. Now, however, I'm left wondering if I might have made a mistake.

"Was someone murdered there?" Matt asks.

I start searching for the relevant folder.

"Not that I'm aware of."

"Did someone die there?"

I turn to him.

"I know someone must have died in pretty much every house in the world," he continues, "but I'm talking about something major."

"I don't know of anything," I say as I restart my search.

"Suicide?"

"Again, I don't really know much about the history of the house at all."

Finding the right folder, I pull it out and carry it over to the desk, where I set it down so that

I can take a look through the papers.

"It's in my son's room."

I look up at him, and in that moment I think back to the strange sensation I experienced in one of the bedrooms at that house. I also can't help remembering the strange behavior of Prudence Barrymore, which I originally wrote off as just the usual teen angst but which I'm now starting to reconsider.

"If it's anything at all, that is," Matt continues. "I feel so dumb right now. You must think I'm a complete idiot, and you certainly don't owe me anything. Not even your time. Diane just begged me to come down and ask if you knew anything, because she figured that you know the local area really well so if anyone was going to have the inside line on that house..."

He pauses, before getting to his feet.

"I've taken up too much of your time already," he adds.

"Not at all," I tell him, and I already know that I can't simply let him walk out of here. "Mr. Hooper, I genuinely don't know anything about the history of your new house, but I've got a certain degree of experience when it comes to these things and I'd be happy to take a look around."

"Experience?"

"How does this evening sound?" I ask. "That gives me time to make a few checks and see what I'm able to come up with." Now it's my turn to pause, and at the back of my mind I already know that there's one other factor that I need to draw into this situation. "And would you mind if I bring someone with me?"

"Bring someone?" He furrows his brow. "Who?"

"Oh, just a friend," I add delicately, even though I know I might be making a huge mistake. "He's forgotten more about the supernatural than most people will ever learn."

CHAPTER THREE

"EXACTLY WHAT AM I doing here again?" Farrar asks as we stand on the doorstep at the Davis Drive house. "I was in the middle of some very important research."

"You were asleep when I looked through the window," I remind him.

"I was resting my eyes and thinking," he says firmly. "You must understand that my work isn't all about charging into situations and coming up with a plan once everything has gone wrong." He takes a moment to adjust his collar. "Sometimes one must simply sit and think, even if that process takes rather a long time."

"I'm not disagreeing with you," I reply as I hear footsteps approaching the door's other side. "I still don't quite understand why you were snoring, though."

Before Farrar can answer, the door swings open and we find ourselves face-to-face with Diane Hooper. Or, rather, with an exhausted woman who – after a couple of seconds – I realize must be Diane, even though she's clearly been through some kind of ordeal since I last saw her. There are dark shadows under her eyes, and even her skin looks somehow grayer as she murmurs something under her breath and steps aside to let us into the house.

"Hi," I say, trying to hide the fact that I'm so taken aback by her appearance. "I hope it's okay that we dropped by like this. Your husband asked if I could take a look round."

"It's fine," she says softly.

As soon as I'm in the hallway, I realize that the house has changed massively. Whereas before this place was bright and airy, now there's a gloomy and closed-off quality to the interior, as if some kind of fog has settled in all the rooms. I turn and look around, and I realize that there's also a strange sense of stillness here, and then I look at Farrar and immediately see that he's noticed something as well. Diane mutters something and slips past us, heading toward the kitchen, and I feel a shiver run through my bones as I realize that the house on Davis Drive now has all the atmosphere of a cemetery.

"This is quite a change," I whisper.

"You were right to bring me," Farrar replies, looking up the stairs for a moment. "Whatever's in this house, evidently it doesn't much mind advertising its presence."

"What do you mean?" I ask.

"I mean that it's sprawling out and making itself feel at home," he explains. "I mean that it almost seems to be enjoying the dourness it brings, and the impact this must be having on the people living here." He stares up at the landing for a few more seconds before turning to me. "It's almost proud of itself," he adds. "This is certainly not a ghost that feels any need to hide."

***

"It started just a day or two after we moved in," Diane says as we sit at the kitchen table. "At first I thought I was just tired from the move, but then I realized that I felt like I was being watched all the time."

"It comes and goes," Matt continues, "but I swear it's like there's someone else here with us. Apart from Diane and me and the kids, that is."

"Have you seen any kind of entity?" I ask.

He shakes his head.

"I thought... maybe," Diane says. "I'm not sure. I was in the laundry room, putting some things in a basket, and out of the corner of my eye I suddenly realized that someone was standing in the doorway." She looks over at the door that leads through to the laundry room. "When I turned to look, it was gone, but no-one else was supposed to be at home with me at the time."

"It sounds so stupid," Matt adds. "When you think of ghosts, you think of them haunting big old houses, or mansions, or places that seem to have a lot of atmosphere. Not laundry rooms in ordinary three-bedroomed houses that were built in the 1970s. That's why we resisted the idea at first. I can't even believe that this house has been standing for long enough to get haunted."

"You never know how things might have worked out," I tell him. "If -"

"Have you heard a voice at all?" Farrar interjects, and I can hear a sense of urgency in his voice.

"Nothing," Diane replies.

"What about your children?" he asks.

"I -"

Diane hesitates. She looks over at her husband, as if for support, and then she turns to us again.

"Katie's doing great," she says cautiously. "She loves living here, she thinks moving away from the city was the best thing we ever did. But her older brother Lance -"

"He's just settling in," Matt says, interrupting her. "There's really nothing to worry about. He's young, and kids go through weird things when they're that age."

"Not like this," Diane says through gritted teeth.

"If we over-analyze him," Matt continues, as they play out an argument that they've clearly gone through already, "we'll just make things worse."

"Whatever's in this house is doing something to Lance," Diane tells me. "My husband doesn't like it when I talk about this, but it's so obvious. He was a happy boy before we moved here, and now he's morose and angry and sometimes I catch him staring at me as if he really hates me." She pauses, and now she has tears in her eyes. "I know you think I've overreacting and I don't blame you for that, but my own son looks at me like he's filled with this... loathing."

"It's not as bad as she makes it sound," Matt says. "But... I have to admit that something's definitely wrong. That's why I dropped by the office today, Ms. Willow. We've tried everything and now we're thinking about ghosts and stuff like that, and we both feel like we're going crazy. I was kind of hoping you might tell me that the previous owners experienced something similar."

"We're not going to sue anyone," Diane adds, and now she seems more desperate than ever. "We just want to know."

"I'm not aware of the previous owners having going through something like this," I tell her, "and as you mentioned, the house is fairly new. It's barely fifty years old. But that doesn't mean that there might not be something going on here. Without going into too much detail, I've encountered things in houses in Candleward before, and I'm very much aware that things can happen that might seem unlikely. I'm no expert, but..."

My voice trails off for a moment as I try to work out how I can make them feel better.

"*I'm* an expert," Farrar says suddenly.

I turn to him.

"I am," he adds, as if he wants to emphasize that point. "I've been studying this sort of thing for most of my life, and I can tell you that I sensed something in this house from the moment I walked through the door. There's some kind of activity here, and the first step is to identify the precise nature of that activity."

He pulls some of his home-made devices from his pocket and sets them on the table. As he mutters to himself and sorts through them, I can't help but notice that his hands are trembling more than ever. I know that Farrar has a great deal of experience, but I'm fully aware that right now he might not be inspiring too much confidence.

"He's really good," I tell the Hoopers. "I promise."

"This might help," Farrar says, holding up a device that looks like a set of paperclips attached to a light-bulb. "In these small rooms, there'll be a concentration of energy and we can use that to our advantage. Of course, these new builds tend to have rather flimsy construction standards. It's not like a good old-fashioned stone house, where the walls are much more solid. Still, we have to work with what we've got."

"Do you really think you can... detect whatever's here?" Diane asks.

"I have absolutely no doubt that we can do that," Farrar tells her, still looking at the various devices. "That's the easy part. The hard part is eradicating the presence, especially if it doesn't *want* to be eradicated. Some of them can be very stubborn, and that's where the difficulty starts." He holds up another device, and I swear his hands are shaking even more. "Knowledge, however, is the key. If one is going into battle, one must know as much as possible about one's enemy. I need to check the rooms upstairs, because I feel that's where the entity is focused. Mercy, while I'm doing that, would you mind talking to the children and trying to get their side of the story? You're better at talking to children than I am. Well, you're better at talking to anyone."

"But you can help us, right?" Diane says, looking at me and then back at Farrar. "You guys know what you're doing, don't you?"

"Sure we do," I tell her, in the absence of any kind of confident statement from my associate. "We're totally on the case."

CHAPTER FOUR

"LANCE IS DIFFERENT," KATIE says a few minutes later, as I sit on a wall in the back garden and watch her playing with some toy cars. She's only eight years old, but I can tell that she understands something's not quite right. "He doesn't play with me like he used to."

"In what way is he different?" I ask.

I wait for an answer, but she seems reluctant to say anything more. After a moment she looks up at me; I'm quite sure that she has things she wants to tell me, but she seems worried about getting into trouble. She turns and looks across the garden, toward the shed where I know Lance is busying himself with some boxes. Is she scared of her brother?

"You can tell me anything," I continue.

"You can even tell me things you haven't told your parents. I'm a friend, and I'm here to see what's going on. Once I've done that, I can hopefully help to make everything better." Again I wait; I can completely understand her nervousness, but I'm going to need a little more information from her before I can move to the next stage of whatever plan Farrar comes up with. "It's not mean of you to tell me things about your brother," I add. "You'll be helping him."

"He calls me names."

"I don't think that's -"

"And sometimes he pinches me. Really hard. And he hits me."

"Where does he hit you?"

She hesitates before touching the side of her arm.

"How hard?" I ask.

She hesitates again, and then she lifts the sleeve of her dress to reveal a couple of large, purplish-yellow bruises.

"Do your parents know about this?" I continue.

She nods.

"They just think we're playing too rough," she says. "Or they did, until the latest one. Now I think they realize he's being too mean, but I don't think they know how to stop him. Sometimes he's mean to them too."

"Does he hit them?"

"Sometimes."

I look back into the house. Matt and Diane are still sitting at the kitchen table, and I have no doubt that their hushed conversation must be about Lance. I'm not surprised at all if they've been holding a few things back, and they must be absolutely terrified, but I need to know what's really going on. And when I turn to Katie again I see that a tear has run down her face. She's just a kid, and the last thing I want to do is push her too far, so after a moment I get to my feet.

"It's going to be okay," I tell her. "Let me just go and talk to your brother for a moment."

***

"Lance?" I say as I stand in the open doorway and look into the shed, where I can just about see a young boy crouching in the darkness and sorting through a few packing boxes. "My name's Mercy. Can I talk to you for a minute or two?"

He doesn't immediately respond. Instead he pulls some old toys out of the box and examines them, before setting them aside on the floor. Only after that does he turn to me, and I can't deny that I feel a shudder run through my bones as I see the angry stare in his eyes. This kid has never met me before and already he looks like he hates me, and I think I'm starting to better understand his mother's concern.

"How are things going?" I ask, trying to sound casual and relaxed. "Are you liking your new home?"

"It's okay," he says softly, before returning his attention to the box.

"Clearing out some stuff, huh?" I continue.

He pulls another toy – some kind of robot – from the box and bangs it down against the floor. I might be getting a little over-sensitive here, but I think he might have slammed the toy down more forcefully, as if to let me know that he'd rather be left alone.

"Moving's hard," I tell him. "I know that the –"

"It's not hard."

"You don't think so?"

"It's just what it is," he adds with a shrug. "It's not like I've got any choice in things, anyway. Mum and Dad told us we're moving, so we moved. No-one cares what I think."

"I'm sure that's not true."

"It's totally true." He holds up another robot, and this one seems to attract his attention a little more than the first. "I'm just a kid. I don't get to make decisions."

"Cornwall's not so bad once you get to know it," I tell him, "and I'm sure you'll make friends once you start at school."

"I don't want to make friends."

"You might find that you make them anyway," I continue. "Trust me, I know from experience that sometimes people just have a way of finding you."

"Lucky you."

"So how are you finding your new room?" I ask, trying to edge closer to the real reason that I'm here. "You've got the room on the left at the top of the stairs, haven't you? The one with the built-in wardrobe?"

"So what?"

"So I'm just wondering whether you like it in there?"

"It's okay."

"Just okay?"

"Do you actually want something?" he asks, turning to me. "I'm busy."

"I think your parents are worried about you, Lance," I continue. "Your sister's worried too. If there's something in that room that's scaring you, you need to let someone know. Someone who'll believe you and who'll help you. That person might not be your parents, because you might not want to upset them, but I'm here and -"

"I know you're here," he snarls, and I'm shocked by the level of anger in his voice. "How could I not know that? You won't stop talking!"

"That's a fair point," I admit.

"If I wanted to talk to anyone about anything," he continues, "then I'm really not short of possibilities. There's my parents, and there's my stupid little sister, and believe it or not in the modern day we have things called phones, so it's not hard to talk to the friends I left behind when we moved." He pauses, still glaring at me as if he's willing me to leave him alone. "I'm fine," he adds. "I'm just looking for some old toys I might be able to sell online so that I can raise some money for a camp I want to go to. Is that really so weird?"

"Not at all," I tell him.

"And you're slowing me down," he adds, as he slams one of the toys back into the box. "These are all broken, anyway. I should never have let Katie play with them. Now they're just junk."

"I hope you find something you can sell," I tell him, as I realize that – for now, at least – I don't seem to have much chance of making progress. "I think I saw that the local paper shop's looking for delivery boys. If you've got a bike, you could always try to earn money that way. I know it sounds old-fashioned, but it's not a bad job."

"Whatever," he mumbles.

Figuring that I'm not going to get much more out of him, I take a step back. I'm not really sure what I was expecting, but so far Lance Hooper seems like a fairly typical – if angry – teen boy.

Sure he talks like someone who's a little older, but I imagine that's due to all the social media these kids consume these days. There's nothing specific that I can point to as a concern, although I realize after a moment that perhaps there's one last thing I should try to ascertain before I head back into the house.

"Lance," I say cautiously, "when you get angry, do you ever lash out?"

"What do you mean?"

"Do you ever take it out on people? For example, do you ever hit your sister? Or even your parents?"

"No!" he replies, as if the idea is ludicrous. In fact, this is the most animated he's seemed since I started talking to him. "Are you mad? I've never hit anyone in my life!"

"That's good to hear," I tell him. "I think I'll leave you alone now."

He doesn't reply, so after a couple of seconds I simply turn and start making my way back across the garden. Katie's still playing near the back door, and although I'm worried about those bruises on her arm, I really don't get the impression that Lance is some kind of monster. In fact, as I step back into the house, I'm starting to wonder whether I've had this whole situation wrong right from the start.

CHAPTER FIVE

"THERE'S SOMETHING IN HERE," Farrar says a few minutes later, as we stand upstairs in the room that once belonged to Prudence Barrymore and which Lance is now making his own. "A kind of unwelcome presence. Can you feel it?"

"It's a teen boy's bedroom," I point out, keeping my voice down a little. "I'm sure there are quite a few unwelcome presences. Don't you remember what it was like when *you* were a teenager?"

"I was never a teenager," he replies, sounding a little offended by the idea. "They hadn't been invented when I was that age. When I was a young man of Lance's age, I was already hard at work as my father's assistant. He was a shoe repairer, and everyone in the family was expected to contribute to the business. His father had been a shoe repairer, as had his father before him. It's shoe repairers all the way back in my family." He glances at me. "Back then, one didn't get asked what one wanted to be when one grew up. One merely joined the family trade, if there was one, or one went and... I don't know, got sent down the mines."

"I guess there's been some progress since then," I suggest.

"Not always for the better," he grumbles, before looking back down at the compass he's been holding for the past few minutes, letting it dangle from a length of string. "This room is the focal point of the entity that's haunting this house, but I haven't been able to get any good readings."

"I can sense something," I tell him. "It's not like Payne Priory, where I couldn't pick up on anything at first."

"This is more present, yet at the same time more diffuse," he explains, turning and looking over at the wardrobe. "The entity is happy to make its presence known, but it seems to be hiding from *me*. The only assumption that makes any sense is that it knows I – or rather, we – pose a threat."

"A threat?"

"It doesn't want to be confronted," he suggests. "It wants to keep the Hooper family to itself. It's simultaneously very brave and direct, yet also cautious. I'm detecting a level of self-awareness that's unusual in ghosts."

"So what do we do about it?" I ask. "Clearly it's ruining the lives of the Hoopers, so we can't just leave it here. Do you want to grab a spirit board and try to talk to the thing? Do you want to find some other way to figure out what it wants? I can research the history of the house and see whether there's anything obvious."

"That's a good idea," he tells me, "but I suspect you'll find nothing."

"Then where did the ghost come from?"

"I have a theory that it might have been here before the house was every built," he explains. "In effect, the house was built around it, and that process might even have helped to focus the ghost's mind a little more strictly. In that case the house has become a kind of cage, and the ghost might very well not be happy about that fact. Tell me, do you know anything about the land that was used for Davis Drive?"

"Just that there were a few controversial building developments back in the sixties and seventies," I tell him. "Obviously that was before my time here, but my understanding is that there's still some ill feeling. Some of the locals think the M.P. at the time was being paid by the developers. It's typical small village politics, but it's amazing how the rancor can linger."

I wait for an answer, but I can tell that

Farrar's worried. After a moment he steps over to the wardrobe and pulls the doors open, but there's nothing in there except a few more of Lance's boxes. A moment later, however, I hear a scuffing sound and I turn to see that Lance himself is watching us from the doorway. Before I have a chance to say anything, I'm struck by the sense that his expression reminds me of the look on Prudence Barrymore's face.

"What are you looking for?" he asks.

"Nothing," I tell him, as Farrar comes over to join me. "In fact, I think we're pretty much done here."

***

"I'm sorry we can't be more specific yet," I tell Matt and Diane as they follow us out to the street. "It's rarely possible to just figure things out after just one visit."

"To be honest," Matt replies, "we were hoping you'd look around and then tell us that we're completely mad."

Farrar and I turn to him.

"But you're not doing that," he continues, "are you?"

"The house is so new," Diane points out. "It was built in 1979, so that's only forty-four years. Is there really time for something bad to have happened here?" She sighs. "I don't even believe in that sort of stuff. Or do I? I'm not even sure."

"We're going to do some research," I tell her, "and then I'll be in touch. We're not going to just walk away and forget about what's going on. We're going to get to the bottom of it."

I pause, waiting for Farrar to chime in, and then I turn to see that he seems lost in thought. I wait a moment longer, and then I gently nudge his arm.

"Hmm?" he replies, having clearly been thinking about something else. "Oh, yes, absolutely. Whatever Mercy just said, I completely agree."

"I was telling them that we're going to come back once we've got some answers," I explain.

"I'm sure we will," he says, before turning to Matt and Diane. "I'm sure Mercy will let you know if we uncover anything."

"What should we do in the meantime?" Diane asks. "Should we try... candles?"

"Candles?" I reply, raising a skeptical eyebrow.

"I don't know, just to... ward off the ghosts or something? I tried to look online but it was really hard to work out what might work and what was just a load of nonsense."

"I think the best thing for now would be to sit tight," I tell her, while secretly hoping that Farrar might have some thoughts. When I glance at him, however, I see that he's once again lost in thought, so I quickly turn to Diane again. "And it's really important to not panic," I continue. "I don't think you're in any immediate danger. Just look after each other and I promise we'll be in touch soon."

After a few more exchanges, Matt and Diane head back inside. Once we're alone, I turn to Farrar and see that he doesn't even seem to have noticed that the Hoopers have left. He only turns to me when I finally clear my throat in an attempt to attract his attention.

"Is everything okay?" he asks.

"Spill."

"I have no idea what you -"

"You're worried about something," I continue, "and I understand why you might have wanted to hide it from the people who are actually living in that house, but I need to know what we're dealing with."

"I have no idea."

"Then why do you look like someone who just uncovered a particularly nasty secret?"

"It's just a theory, that's all," he replies defensively, "and I simply can't discuss it until I've done a little more work and tried to uncover the truth."

"But -"

"And you won't get anything else out of me by nagging," he adds, "so please, don't even try. I'm sorry, Mercy, but I like to move slowly and I can assure you that as soon as I have anything to reveal, you'll be the first to know. The last thing I want to do is add fuel to the fire or lead us down the wrong path. My suggestion is that while I do some reading, you need to find out about this patch of land. Don't focus too much on the house, try to see if the land has any kind of history. And above all, keep an open mind."

I want to ask more questions, but he seems agitated and I can tell that he won't react well. Whenever Farrar starts to go into his own head like this, I know the best thing is simply to let him get on with things, so instead I start leading him toward the car. As I unlock the doors, however, I can't help glancing back at the house and thinking about the Hoopers. Something in that building is draining them, and I'm fairly sure that it was draining Prudence Barrymore when she lived there too. I can't shake the feeling that this might be a ghost unlike any other I've encountered.

CHAPTER SIX

ONCE I'VE DROPPED FARRAR off at Torfork Tower, I head into town on a mission to discover more about Davis Drive. Or rather, as Farrar keeps insisting, about the land that Davis Drive occupies, since he seems certain that this is going to throw up more answers than any other research. Part of me worries that he's simply trying to distract me, but I tell myself that a little research is never a bad idea.

I head, of course, to the library. This place has become almost my home away from home in Candleward, although this time I don't simply head straight for the computers in the reference section. Instead I ask the man at the desk about any land registry information, and he seems positively thrilled to lead me down some stairs into a part of the library that most people don't even know is here.

This is a world of low ceiling and poor lighting, and I have to duck down a little as I follow him toward a door at the far end of one of the corridors.

"I hope I'm not disturbing you," I tell him.

"Don't be silly. We're rarely run off our feet at the library these days, more's the pity. We have to complete regular logs to tell the bean-counters how many people are using our facilities. Your visit will be another entry in the plus column as far as they're concerned."

"I don't know what I'd do without this place."

"You should find everything you're looking for in here," he tells me as he reaches the door and grabs the handle. "It's strange, no-one's been to use this part of the collection for the best part of ten years, and then what happens? Two show up on the same day!"

"Two?" I ask.

As soon as he opens the door, I can't help but let out a sigh as I see Mr. Allen standing at a desk with a large map laid out. He turns to me, and to be honest I think he sighs too.

"Do you two happen to know each other?" the librarian asks, having clearly clocked our reactions. "Are you... friends?"

***

"Like I explained," I continue a few minutes later, as I pull out a large folder and set it on one of the other desks, "I'm here to check out some maps of Candleward from back in the day."

I glance at him.

"Isn't that exactly what *you're* doing?" I ask.

"Absolutely," he replies, wandering over to join me, "but I'm working in pursuit of a better understanding of my family's history. I have a long-term project on the go, whereas your frequent trips to the library seem to be driven by some other impulse entirely." He looks down at the map. "What are you trying to find out?"

I want to tell him that it's none of his business, but I know that won't work. He seems driven to constantly stick his nose into everyone else's business, so I simply roll out the map to reveal an illustration showing Candleward as it existed back in the year 1887. I quickly spot the location that's now Davis Drive, but to my disappointment I see that it's just marked as a section of bare land, with no interesting labels at all. I know I was being too optimistic when I hoped that I'd find it was some abandoned cemetery, but I can't deny that I feel a little disappointed.

"Candleward was much smaller back then, wasn't it?" Mr. Allen observes.

"It's small now," I counter.

"Yes, but it was absolutely tiny in the

nineteenth century," he continues. "By those standards, these days it's almost a teeming metropolis."

"Have you ever been to a teeming metropolis?" I ask, turning to him.

"Have you?"

"Candleward isn't teeming," I continue, as I put the map away, "and it's definitely not a metropolis. I'm sorry, I don't mean to be rude, it's just that I need to find out what used to be on the site of Davis Drive."

"Davis Drive?"

"You know where I mean?" I reply as I grab another map and see that this one is from 1751. I doubt there'll be anything of interest here, but I roll it out anyway. "It's not too far from here."

"I remember the fuss when they built those houses," he mutters, and he – like so many people in Candleward – still seems annoyed. "It's not the best land, you know. It'd flood if it wasn't so high up."

"So you're saying it doesn't flood?"

"But it would! If it could!"

"There's still nothing here," I remark as I examine this latest map. I've already got a sinking feeling, but I know I need to be thorough so I roll the map up and grab another, which turns out to be from 1672. "I'm surprised they even have copies of these maps," I continue. "This one's from more than three hundred years ago."

"The Candleward Library Trust has been very focused on digitizing its assets," Mr. Allen tells me. "I'd venture to say that we're far ahead of most other libraries in the country."

"And I'll be forever grateful," I tell him as I look at the map, "but I don't think -"

Stopping suddenly, I see that this particular map is a little different to the others. This time, while there's no text anywhere near the Davis Drive area, I spot what appears to be a very deliberate little mark. Peering closer, I try to make out whether the mark has any distinguishing features, but it appears to be simply a short vertical straight line. My first thought is that it might just be a scrap of damage, but as I peer more intently I realize that this mark certainly appears to have been left deliberately, although I have no idea what it might represent.

"What do you make of that?" I ask.

"Make of what?" he replies, leaning over next to me and adjusting his glasses as he too examines the map.

"That mark there," I continue. "You don't think it's..."

I pause, before turning to him.

"You don't think it could be a cemetery, do you?"

"Out there? Under Davis Drive?"

"It'd explain a few things."

"Like what?"

"Like..." I stop myself just in time. "Like some subsidence that one of the houses has been experiencing. That's all."

"So this is a structural investigation, is it?"

"In a manner of speaking."

He looks at the map again, and he seems momentarily lost in thought.

"No," he says finally, "I don't think that's a cemetery. I've seen cemeteries on these old maps and they tend to be set out very clearly. I don't think anyone wanted there to be any possibility of a mistake."

I wait for him to continue, in the hope that he might suddenly come up with an answer. After a few more seconds, however, I look back down at the map, and for the first time I realize that the mark appears to have a small horizontal section at the top. Peering even more closely, I have to squint to make out the detail, but I think I'm slowly starting to form a decent guess as to what I'm seeing.

"Hang on," I whisper, "I think this might be -"

"Gallows," Mr. Allen says darkly.

I turn to him.

"It stands to reason," he continues, "that a village like Candleward would have to have an execution site. After all, we're in Cornwall, there's been a massive smuggling presence here for centuries. They weren't big on long trials back in the old days, they tended to march their prisoners straight to the hangman."

"*More* hanging?" I reply, thinking back to the tale of Ronald Beecham at Payne Priory. "You wait all your life for one, and then another comes along shortly after."

"I think it's settled," Mr. Allen says as he prods the map with the tip of a finger. "When Davis Drive was first earmarked for development, a lot of local busybodies got rather agitated about the plight of some rare newt that was said to live on the site. That's what really caused all the problems, but I'm starting to think that the real issue might have been something far more macabre."

"I really don't want to believe that this is true," I tell him.

"What you want isn't relevant, is it?" he replies, as we both continue to stare down at the map. "Based on this, it would appear that Davis Drive was built directly on the site of the old Candleward gallows." He sighs. "I reckon there might be rather a lot of ghosts knocking about that area. Don't you?"

CHAPTER SEVEN

"GALLOWS," FARRAR MURMURS AS he stares down at the copy I made of the map. "Well, that would be a turn up for the books, wouldn't it?"

"I cross-referenced the idea with some other books," I explain. We're standing in the tower room at Torfork Tower, with a nearby candle flickering in the darkness. Apparently he's trying to save money on his electricity bill. "From what I can tell, this really *was* the part of Candleward where pirates and other criminals were executed."

"So much negative energy building up in one location," he mutters. "And then someone built houses all over the site, trapping the ghosts. I'm surprised more people on that development haven't reported ghostly presences."

"What do we do?" I ask, struggling to see

where we can go from here. "Assuming that the ghost on Davis Drive is someone who was executed years ago, are we supposed to somehow set her spirit to rest?" I pause for a moment as I think of the various possibilities. "This isn't going to be like Payne Priory again, is it?"

"No, this is nothing like Payne Priory," he says firmly. "I can tell that already."

"Then what -"

"Perhaps there's nothing we *can* do," he adds, before shuffling over to one of the other desks. "I've said it before, Mercy, and I'll say it again. We can't help everyone."

"But -"

"I'm an old man," he points out. "I don't have many years left, so I have to prioritize which cases I take on and which I pass over." He picks up one of his old notebooks, and once again I'm struck by his frailty as his hands tremble wildly. Frankly, I'm surprised he can even read that notebook right now. "I don't have the luxury of wasting time on minor issues."

"Minor issues?"

I wait for a reply, but he's making a point of leafing through the notebook, as if he really wants me to accept that he won't be offering any more help. I want to ask him what's wrong, but I know there's no way he'll be honest with me. Farrar's one of the nicest people I've ever met, yet in some ways he very much keeps himself to himself.

"Are you still here?" he asks finally.

"I want to know how to help the Hoopers," I tell him.

"You could always put the house back on the market."

"But then someone else would move in and the same thing would happen," I continue. "You didn't meet Prudence Barrymore, but she was clearly dealing with the same entity. She was angry and morose all the time, and I'm pretty sure that at least once I overheard her talking to someone in her bedroom. Whatever's in that house, it's clearly messing with everyone who lives there and I don't think it'll ever stop."

"Then don't stop it."

I open my mouth to reply, but holding back as I realize the enormity of what he just said.

"Mercy," he says, clearly in some degree of discomfort, "when I moved down to Candleward, I never intended to become part of some little team that goes around fixing the problems of unimportant little people like Matt and Diane Hooper. Whatever's going on in that house, it doesn't matter, not in the grand scheme of things. I have important work to do, and I don't have enough time in which to do it, so while I enjoy your company I must beg you to leave me alone for a little while." He glances at me. "I'm sorry if that sounds harsh, but it's the truth. I spent a lot of time with you at Payne Priory, and I simply don't have the energy to get involved with such things too often. Please try to understand."

"Of course," I reply, even though I'm shocked by his attitude. "I didn't mean to intrude."

"Today I'm researching some particularly interesting -"

"I should go," I add, turning and hurrying out of the room. "I've got so much work to do before I even think about heading back to Davis Drive."

He calls after me, but I don't even slow my pace as I head down the stairs. Something about Farrar's tone made me feel as if I've misjudged this whole situation, as if I was wrong to think that he might be becoming a friend. And by the time I get outside and stop to take a deep breath, I've already reminded myself that I never came to Cornwall to make friends at all; I came to start a new life, and I seem to have developed a sideline in dealing with ghosts, but I really don't need to start making strong connections.

After all, there's always a chance I might one day have to leave without a moment's notice.

***

"No, I'm not trying to sell anything," I continue,

trying my very best to seem friendly and approachable. "It's more of a... research project."

I'm standing at the first house on Davis Drive, conducting a somewhat ill-thought-out and under-prepared survey. Having taken another look at a map of the area, I came to the conclusion that Davis Drive winds its way gently uphill around a part of the landscape that somewhat stands out from the edge of a nearby forest; having taken that into account, I'm fairly sure that I understand why this would have been a good place to locate the local gallows, in which case I'm trying to understand whether it's *only* the Hoopers' house that's impacted by any ghostly activity. If people were being executed here a few hundred years ago, then it stands to reason that any strange presences should be at least somewhat shared by several of the properties.

"And you want to know about ghosts?" the man at the door replies, clearly already somewhat skeptical.

"It's an odd research project," I continue, trying to strike a conciliatory tone. "I'm from a university program over near Truro and we're look into patterns of belief in the supernatural."

As I wait for him to reply, I realize that my explanation actually sounded quite good. Perhaps I missed my true calling as a researcher after all.

"I mean," the man says cautiously, "if you're

asking whether we've seen any ghosts while we've been living here, then the answer's definitely no."

"I see."

"I don't know what else to tell you," he adds with a shrug. "If you want to leave a card, I can get in touch if I suddenly spot a floating bed-sheet on the landing one night."

"No, it's fine, thank you," I reply, already taking a step back. "I'm sorry to have bothered you."

"Are you sure I can't take a card?"

I hesitate for a moment, before pulling one of my cards from my pocket and handing it to him. I guess it can't hurt to maybe give him a way of contacting me later if something comes up.

"An estate agent, huh?" he suggests, raising an eyebrow. "And you claim you're not selling anything? Sure."

Before I can answer and try to defend myself, he shuts the door.

"Damn it," I mutter under my breath, although I don't blame him for his reaction. "This is starting to feel like a real fool's errand."

Once I've finished at the first house, I make my way up the street, trying each door – except number three, for obvious reasons – and coming up with absolutely nothing. I don't get many people to answer their doors at all, presumably because the majority of the occupants are out at work, and the few who *do* answer seem very uninterested in my so-called project. And as I step away from the very last house and stop to look back down the hill, I can't say that I blame anyone for thinking that I might be a little crazy. There are twenty houses on Davis Drive and as far as I can tell, number three is the only one that's exhibiting any sign of ghostly activity. If that activity had started after the Hoopers moved in, I could maybe chalk it up to their children being particularly imaginative, but I keep coming back to the fact that Prudence Barrymore also showed signs of a paranormal encounter.

From where I'm standing, I can see the Hoopers' house. Their back garden backs onto a gently sloping grassy hill that runs up toward the edge of the forest, and now I find myself wondering *exactly* where the old gallows might have stood. At the moment I'm flying blind, and I feel as if there's a large part of the historical record that I'm missing. I'm used to going back a century, sometimes a little more, to figure out what's going on with a property, but this time something tells me that I'm going to have to delve much further into Candleward's past if I'm ever going to figure out what really happened here.

Long before this hill was Davis Drive, it was clearly something much darker. Unfortunately, I'm worried that part of that past is now leaking into the present day.

CHAPTER EIGHT

"IT'S HONESTLY NOTHING SERIOUS," I say as I sit at my dining room table and look at the laptop's screen. "I just really wanted to ask a few follow-up questions about your recent move."

"Uh... sure," Doug Barrymore replies, his face briefly becoming a little pixellated over the video call. "I should tell you that I think dinner's going to be ready soon so -"

"I won't keep you for very long," I continue, already aware that I'm overstepping so many boundaries here. "I promise."

As those words leave my lips, I feel a paw on my leg. Looking down, I see that Miss Chloe has brought her favorite toy over for me to throw; I take it from her mouth and toss it across the room, and then I turn to the screen again. Rain is hammering the window next to me as a storm moves in for the night.

"Sorry," I add. "My dog has chosen this exact moment to try to get playtime started. I think it might be because of the bad weather."

"You said you wanted to talk to Prudence, right?"

"If that's okay."

"Let me take the laptop through to her," he continues, and the image on the screen swings wildly as he gets to his feet and starts heading through to another part of their new house. "Prue? There's someone here who'd like a quick word with you, if that's okay?"

I can hear them talking quietly off-camera, so I take a moment to get myself ready. Miss Chloe hurries over and I have to throw her toy giraffe again, and a moment later the image on the screen shifts again and I find myself face-to-face – digitally speaking, of course – with Prudence Barrymore. Before I have a chance to say anything, however, I'm shocked to see that she looks so different: whereas before she had a pale, very withdrawn countenance, now she looks happy and healthy, as if she's experience a remarkable turnaround.

"Hi," I say, unable to hide a sense of surprise.

"Hi," she replies, clearly somewhat taken

aback. "You're... that estate agent, right?"

"I am," I tell her. "I don't know what your father told you, but I just have a few questions about the time when you were living here in Candleward. Specifically about your bedroom in the house at Davis Drive."

She visibly stiffens as soon as I mention that room. She looks to her left, as if she's worried about being overhead, and then she switches chairs as if she wants to get as far away from her parents as possible.

"I've been trying to figure out how to say this delicately," I continue, "but I'm not sure how to be -"

"Is it still there?" she asks, cutting me off.

"Is *what* still there?"

He hesitates, and I can tell that she's reluctant to talk to me.

"Anything you tell me," I add, "will stay just between the two of us."

She looks around again, and then she moves the laptop closer to her face.

"I didn't really know what was going on at the time," she whispers. "I guess it almost felt normal, in a strange way. But when we moved, after I got used to being in this new house, I realized how screwy everything had been in Candleward." She pauses again. "There's something in that house. In my old room. I don't know what it was, but it talked to me sometimes, mainly at night. Please, don't tell my parents that I'm saying any of this, I don't want them to get me put on medication."

"I won't tell a soul."

"I still don't even know if it was real," she continues, "but it felt like... something was living in the wardrobe."

"Specifically in the wardrobe?"

She nods.

"Okay," I say after a moment, as I try to make sense of what she's telling me. "And what did this... thing in the wardrobe do?"

"She talked to me."

"She?"

"I think it was female," she explains, and now she seems to be becoming increasingly agitated. "I don't know, now that I'm away from it, the whole thing feels totally crazy. But at the time, I was having these long, hushed conversations with some kind of thing that lived in my room. Most of the time it was just a voice, but sometimes at night it'd come out and I'd try to hide, but I'd peek sometimes and I'd see this figure moving in the darkness."

"You think there's a ghost in your old room?"

"I think there's definitely something," she continues. She looks around again, as if she's still terrified that her parents might overhear. "It took over my life for a while, and it was always telling me to do bad things. Like... *really* bad things. The worst things you could ever imagine."

"Can you give me some examples?"

"Think of the worst things ever," she says, lowering her voice even further, until I can barely hear her at all, "and then think worse than that. It was like she really wanted to make me suffer, like she wanted us all to be in pain. The worst part is..."

I wait, but she seems unable to finish that sentence.

"I nearly did it," she adds finally, as I see tears in her eyes. "I nearly did what she wanted, and I never would have been able to forgive myself. And when Dad said we were moving, for some reason I was actually angry! I didn't want to be taken away from that room, because for some ridiculous reason I thought the *thing* in there could teach me." She shakes her head. "It all sounds so crazy now, I can't even believe that it actually happened. I'm just glad that I got away before..."

Again I wait, but she seems lost in her own thoughts now.

"Prue?" Misha's voice suddenly calls out in the background of the call. "Dinner's on the table!"

"I have to go," Prudence says hurriedly.

"Wait, I think -"

"I'm fine now," she adds, glaring into the lens of her laptop's camera. "You don't need to call again. Please don't try. I'm sorry, I just want to forget that any of that stuff ever happened. And if anyone's in that room now, tell them to get out before..."

She hesitates, and then with no further warning she cuts the call. My first thought is that I should try to call her back and get some more information, but to be honest I think she wants to firmly forget about her time at that house, and I don't blame her one bit. In fact, I'm already starting to think that Farrar and I might have underestimated the danger posed by that place.

***

By the time I get back to Davis Drive and knock on the door of number three, rain is falling harder and harder. At least I have a raincoat to keep my dry, with the hood pulled up and tied tight under my chin.

"Ms. Willow?" Matt says as soon as he opens the door. "It's late, what are you -"

"You need to get out of this house," I tell him.

"I'm sorry?"

"Just as a precaution," I continue, raising my voice a little as I'm almost drowned out by the sound of rain hitting my hood. "Just until we can be sure that it's safe."

"This is our home," he points out.

"I know, but -"

"And I've got work tomorrow," he adds. "So does my wife."

"Yes, but if -"

"What do you want us to do, go and live in a hotel for a while?"

"That might not be a bad idea."

"And who's going to pay for that?" he continues. "You?"

I open my mouth to tell him that he has to do whatever it takes, but at the last second I realize that he might have a point. I came racing over here so fast, I didn't stop to think about the practical consequences of what I was planning to tell him.

"Who is it?" his wife calls out from upstairs.

"No-one!" he shouts back at her. "I'll be up in a minute!"

"I know you must think I'm crazy," I continue, "and to be honest, I hope you're right. But I spoke to someone tonight who used to live here, and from what she told me, I don't think it's safe for you to be here right now. In particular, I don't think your son should be in that room."

"I came to you for help," he replies, "not just to be told to get out of the house I only just bought."

"It's not as simple as waving a few crucifixes around or bringing in a priest to banish whatever's here," I tell him, "although both of those options might be worth trying. The point is, we need to proceed cautiously, and that means getting you out of here until we come up with a better plan."

"And as I've already told you, we don't have that luxury." He stares at me for a moment, almost as if he's angry. "I think the best thing might be for you to just leave us alone. I'm sorry we came to you, it was a moment of weakness but it won't happen again and -"

"What about the bruises on Katie's arm?" I ask.

"What bruises?"

"You must have seen them," I continue, trying to think of anything that might make him come around to my way of thinking. "Something's trying to hurt her."

"Now you're starting to offend me," he replies firmly. "Are you seriously suggesting that my wife and I wouldn't know if someone was attacking our children?"

"I -"

"Do you have any children, Ms. Willow?"

"No," I lie, although I immediately feel unsettled by the question.

"Then stay out of our lives," he adds, mustering a sudden sense of anger that seems at odds to the way he behaved when he came to me for help. "I'm sorry if we gave you the wrong impression and made you think that we want you sticking your nose in, but I really don't think there's anything else you can do for us. Please don't keep knocking on our door, because at some point I'll start to consider that a form of harassment."

Before I can reply and insist that I really only want to help, he swings the door shut with considerable force, as if he wants to make doubly sure that I get the message. With rain still falling all around, I watch as the house's hallway lights are switched off and I can't help but feel that something significant has changed since the last time I was here. If I didn't know better, I'd be inclined to think that Matt Hooper almost seemed like a completely different person.

CHAPTER NINE

ONE HOUR LATER, HUDDLED under a tree on the hill that overlooks Davis Drive, I look through the rain and watch the back window of number three.

Matt Hooper is in the kitchen, doing something at the sink, while Diane's putting things away behind him and the two children are sitting at the table. So far, I haven't noticed anything particularly unusual; in fact, I know that *I'm* the one being a little weird here, since I'm watching the family without their knowledge. At the same time, I can't shake the feeling that something was really wrong with Matt, and I figure that there's no harm in keeping an eye on the family for a short while.

I check my phone; I should be getting home, but I need to know what's going on at the Hoopers' house.

After a few more minutes, Matt disappears from the window and I'm left watching the rest of the Hoopers. Seconds later, however, one of the lights switches on upstairs and I see Matt heading into Lance's bedroom. He stops and looks toward the wardrobe, and I feel a flicker of fear in my chest as I realize that he appears to be waiting for something – or possibly even listening to someone. I tell myself that I'm most likely imagining things, but he certainly appears to paying attention to some force that's just out of my field of vision.

And his family members, meanwhile, are all still downstairs.

"What are you doing?" I whisper as I continue to watch him. "Why -"

Before I can finish, I realize that his lips are moving. I'm fairly sure he's not on the phone; instead, he's simply staring at the wardrobe as he speaks, and now I'm really starting to worry that something's very wrong. I don't want to panic, and I know I can't just go barging back down to their front door and demand to know what's going on, but I'm convinced now that something's very wrong in that house, and that the source of the problem is definitely focused on the wardrobe in that particular room.

"Hurry!" a voice shouts suddenly, ringing out through the dark night and the rain. "Let's not waste more time on this vagabond!"

Startled, I get to my feet and turn around. The voice seemed to be coming from somewhere higher up, perhaps even in the forest, but I have no idea why anyone would be out here so late. Anyone apart from some lunatic estate agent spying on a family, that is. A moment later, however, I hear the sound of footsteps hurrying through the darkness, and those footsteps seem to be echoing all around me; a few seconds after that, something hard and heavy bumps against my shoulder as it passes, and as I turn again I realize I can see the silhouettes of several figures moving through the night.

And a set of gallows towering high above me.

Stepping back, I tell myself that the gallows weren't there a moment ago. They are now, however, and I find myself staring at a high wooden platform with a single plank rising higher up. In the darkness, with rain still falling heavily, I'm just about able to make out a rope hanging from the top of the plank, dangling down with a noose tied at its lower end. At the same time, I feel the air turn noticeably colder, and after a few more seconds I realize I can hear more and more grunts and shouts coming from the darkness all around.

"If you won't give us your name," a man snarls nearby, "then you'll die without one, and you'll be buried in a pit."

"Go to Hell!" another man hisses.

A moment later I hear a loud thudding sound, accompanied by a cry of pain. As I look the other way, I realize I can just about make out dark shapes moving in the night, heading toward the gallows. Finally I watch as several of these shapes start walking up a set of steps and onto the platform beneath the rope. Now I can see the outlines of half a dozen men, and I watch in horror as they quickly put the noose around the neck of their prisoner.

"We don't treat smugglers well in these parts," one of the men mutters. "You should have known that before you came here. Your friends left, didn't they? They ran for their lives and abandoned you, and now you're going to pay the price for all their crimes as well as your own."

"I'm just an honest man," the prisoner stammers, "and -"

"Honest?"

One of the men punches him, sending him falling back until the noose tightens around his neck.

"There's not an honest bone in your body," the first man says firmly. "You're a sniveling wretch and you'll die like an animal. Usually I'd ask for a man's last words, but in this case I don't think I care to hear your voice again."

"You have this all wrong," the prisoner replies, barely able to get any words out. "My crew are honest, we were simply transporting items for a merchant and -"

"In the middle of the night?" the first man asks, clearly amused by this excuse. "Trying to evade notice? You take us for fools."

"Let's get this over with," one of the others mutters. "It's cold out here tonight."

"Hang the bastard," the first man replies.

Before I can react, a hatch opens on the platform and the condemned man drops down. I hear him let out a gasp as the noose pulls tight, but to my horror he struggles as he dangles. A moment later two of the men grab his legs and start pulling, trying to break his neck.

"Stop!" I call out, hurrying toward them. "Wait, you can't do this!"

Suddenly one of the figures turns and glares at me. Spotting two dark, angry eyes burning in the night air, I instinctively pull back and lose my footing. I tumble down and land hard against the grass, and as rain continues to fall all around me I watch as the men continues to pull on their prisoner's legs. I hear a splitting sound, and after a few more seconds the men release the prisoner, leaving him to dangle dead from the gallows.

"A fine night's work," the first man says, clearly satisfied by everything I've just witnessed. "We'll leave him up here for a few days, as fair warning for anyone else who might like to try their hand at smuggling. As God is my witness, I won't stand for this behavior in Candleward. I'll root it out wherever it might hide."

"The world's better off without this sniveling coward," one of the other men remarks, before stepping forward and spitting on the hanging corpse.

"Spread the word through the village," the first man says as they all turn and start traipsing away through the night, heading down the hill toward Candleward. "There's no hiding place here for wickedness. Sadly I doubt the lesson will be so easily learned. I'm quite sure that before too long, we'll be back here again with yet another wretch."

As their footsteps fade away, I'm left staring up at the dead man. I can only see him silhouetted against the dark night sky, but after a few seconds I slowly get to my feet. Almost slipping on the wet grass, I cautiously approach the edge of the gallows. Reaching out, I touch the wood and find that it's surprisingly firm and cold. I make my way around to the other side, and then I start walking up the creaking steps that lead onto the platform. With each step, I half expect the entire apparition to fade away to nothing, but finally I find myself standing on the platform and staring at the dead man. I reach out again, and I have to admit that I feel a shudder pass through my bones as soon as I feel his arm.

His body is still twisting slightly, causing

the rope to let out a faint creaking sound.

Suddenly filled with the sense that I shouldn't be here, I step back and make my way down onto the grass. I blink, and in an instant the gallows disappear entirely. I reach out, just to check that the entire wooden structure is gone, and then I hesitate for a moment as rain continues to batter the hood of my coat. I'm used to seeing ghosts, of course, but somehow this felt different, almost as if I was briefly transported back to the day of a hanging. When I saw ghostly figures at Payne Priory, they seemed almost like projections, whereas the men who surrounded me tonight felt much more real.

I need to ask Farrar about this whole mess.

Turning to look back at the houses, I'm shocked to see a figure stumbling toward me through the darkness.

"I'm no smuggler!" the dead man gasps, grabbing my shoulders and leaning close. "You have to believe me! As God is my witness -"

"Let go of me!" I shout, pulling away and turning to run, only to trip and fall.

Although I try to stop myself hitting the ground too hard, my head smashes against something solid and I'm immediately knocked out cold.

AMY CROSS

CHAPTER TEN

"ALFIE? NOW WHAT HAVE you found there?"

As soon as my eyes open, I notice two things: first, the rain has stopped, and second early morning light is spreading across the village. I blink a couple of times, and then a dog leans down and licks my cheek.

Gasping, I roll onto my back and look up just as a woman peers down at my face.

"Are you okay?" she asks.

"Yes!" I blurt out, before sitting up. I put my hands on the grass to support myself, and I realize that I might have been unconscious for several hours.

"You look like you've hurt yourself."

Reaching up, I touch the side of my forehead and feel a sharp pain. When I look at my fingertips, I spot a few traces of blood. Looking around at the grass, I quickly spot a small section of wood jutting out of the ground, rising perhaps a few inches from the soil. I reach out and touch the wood; this must be what caused the cut on my head as I fell, and a moment later I realize that most likely I've found the remains of the gallows that once stood on this site.

"Are you concussed?" the woman asks. "Do you need me to call a doctor?"

"No!" I reply, stumbling to my feet. "No, honestly, I'm fine."

"Are you sure? Have you been out all night? There was a terrible storm, you'll be lucky if you don't catch pneumonia!"

Checking my watch, I realize that I've lost quite a hefty chunk of time. I'm cold and wet, but as I look down at the houses on Davis Drive I remember the sight of Matt Hooper seemingly talking to someone or something in one of the upstairs rooms. There's no sign of anyone now, but I can't shake the feeling that Matt's behavior was extremely strange. I reach into my pocket to grab my phone, only to find that it's missing.

"Have you seen a phone?" I ask, looking around, worried that it must have fallen out at some point during the night.

"I don't think so," the woman replies, as her dog lifts its leg and pees on the remains of the old gallows. "I hope it hasn't got wet."

"Me too," I say, stepping past her and looking around again. "I really don't know where it can be."

"Are you *sure* you don't need a doctor?" the woman asks. "You really shouldn't ignore head wounds, you know. It's best to get these things checked out, even if you think you're okay."

"Yes, definitely," I reply, still trying to spot my phone. "I'm sorry, thanks for your concern, but I need to be somewhere right now."

***

"Miss Chloe!" I say, mustering as much excitement as possible. "I'm so sorry, I didn't mean to leave you home alone all night! Were you okay?"

As she jumps up for me to give her a fuss, I glance around and see – to my relief – that there don't seem to be any wees or poos anywhere. I have to admit, this dog seems to have an iron bladder.

"Okay, we're going to go for a walk soon," I continue as I step past her and head over to the table, "but I just need to do a couple of things first."

She barks, and I know I'm being desperately unfair to her. In fact, as I sit down and open my laptop, I'm already starting to think that it's time to see whether Nathan and Lily *really* want to adopt her as their own. We've been discussing the possibility for a while, but Nathan seems reluctant to commit and in some ways I can understand why; at the same time, as much as I love having a dog, deep down I know that I'm not really in a position to give her the love and attention she deserves. She's a lovely little girl and she needs a better home.

"I don't understand what's happened to my phone," I say as I open a browser window and navigate to the site that I use for tracking. "You're so lucky, Miss Chloe. Sometimes I think humans would be much happier if phones were still just attached to walls in houses."

I click to find my phone, and as I wait for the signal to show up I can't help thinking back to the sight of those gallows during the night. Somehow the past came to life right before my eyes; I could see and hear the ghosts, but I also felt the wood of the platform. Can inanimate objects also return to haunt the living? I have to admit, I really don't understand the science behind ghosts at all, and I keep hoping that Farrar might be able to help me figure that part out, although in all honesty I'm not sure that he's got much more of an idea.

A green dot appears on the screen. I immediately see that my phone is somewhere near Davis Drive. As I zoom closer, however, I'm shocked to see the exact location.

Miss Chloe barks again.

"Hang on," I tell her, peering closer at the

screen. "How is that possible?"

I remember checking the time on my phone last night, shortly before I got knocked out. As far as I'm aware, I spent several hours unconscious on the grass, but now to my horror I see that my phone is located inside the Hoopers' house on Davis Drive. There's no way I went in there after I saw the gallows last night, so how has my phone managed to make the journey?

For a moment, I imagine myself knocked out on the grass in the dark and the rain. In my mind's eye, I see a figure crouching down and taking my phone, and then the figure turns and walks away, leaving me unconscious.

"That can't have happened," I whisper, although I know there's no other way that my phone could possibly have ended up inside that house. "Who would do that? And why?"

***

"Cards on the table," I say a short while later, as I sit at the kitchen table in Nathan's house. "Do you want a dog?"

He opens his mouth to reply, and then he hesitates for a moment.

"She's cute," I continue, as Miss Chloe runs past with Lily just a few paces behind. "Lily could learn a lot about responsibility if she starts looking after her. You've always said that you want her to learn that sort of thing. And she's clearly off to a good start."

"A dog's a big deal, though," he points out, setting two cups of tea on the table between us before sitting down. "Then again, with three of us living here now, she wouldn't have to be alone too often."

I feel my heart skip a beat.

"Three?"

"Sophia," he replies, and now I can tell that he's feeling somewhat awkward. "Didn't I mention that? It made no sense having her run back and forward between my place and her flat, and once her lease came up we decided that she might as well move in."

"That's great," I say, trying to hide the fact that I absolutely hate the idea. Not that I have any right to feel that way, of course. "Congratulations."

"Do you think it's too fast?"

"Not if it's the right thing to do."

"I don't want to make the situation unstable for Lily," he continues, as we both hear his daughter calling out to Miss Chloe in the garden. "Ordinarily I'd never have asked Sophia to move in so early in our relationship, but the stars just seemed to align that way and fate seemed to be pushing us so... I kind of surprised myself by blurting the question out before I'd thought it through properly."

"And how do you feel now?"

"I feel good," he tells me. "I just worry that I shouldn't."

"Don't second guess yourself too much," I say as I check my watch again. When I look back at Nathan, I can see the doubt in his eyes. "You deserve to be happy."

"So do you," he replies. "Are you sure you're ready to give up Miss Chloe? Won't your place feel too empty?"

"I'm used to that."

"Why?"

"I just don't have the kind of lifestyle that works in a relationship," I tell him, before realizing that I'm getting dangerously close to going into far too much detail. "Trust me, I'm not trying to sound mysterious," I continue, "but my life's a little chaotic. I've tended to bounce around from one place to another, sometimes without much warning."

"Are you thinking of leaving Candleward?"

"No!" I reply, perhaps a little too quickly. "Not at the moment," I add, while checking my watch again, and then I get to my feet. "Listen, I'm sorry, but I really have to be somewhere. Horace has about a million jobs lined up for me and I'm already falling behind. I don't think I can stay for that cup of tea after all."

"But -"

"So are you going to keep Miss Chloe?" I ask. "At least for a test run?"

"For a test run," he replies with a sigh, and I can tell that he's not entirely convinced. "I reserve the right to send her back to you, though. I'm not certain that Lily's ready for a dog." He pauses for a moment. "And Mercy," he adds, "I'm really glad that we can be friends again."

"Of course," I reply, checking my watch for the umpteenth time. "I just -"

"After the kiss, I mean."

I open my mouth to reply, and then I freeze as I feel every muscle in my body tighten. Staring at him for a moment, I'm honestly not sure whether I actually heard what I think I heard. I know that I must look like a complete idiot right now, and I have to say something eventually, but for a few more agonizing seconds I feel as if my brain is about to explode.

"I'm sorry," I say finally, my voice tighten with tension, "but did you just say... kiss?"

CHAPTER ELEVEN

"JESSICA, WHAT DID YOU do? What the hell did you get up to during those six months you had control of our body, and why didn't you tell me about things like kissing Nathan? Are you completely out of your mind?"

Stopping at my car, I realize that I already know the answer to those questions. After all, Nathan just referred to the time recently when – unbeknownst to me – Jessica apparently used my body to kiss him. According to his version of the story, Jessica showed up at his house late one night after a few glasses of wine, and then she let herself in and gave him a very passionate kiss before running out again. The next day she arranged to meet him at a cafe and told him that the whole thing had been a mistake, but I'm still fuming that she never mentioned any of this to me. Nathan seems to have accepted that it was just a one-off drunken incident, and I think I covered my ignorance well enough, but I still feel as if I want to scream.

"I mean it," I say, as I unlock the car door and climb into the driver's seat. "You're going to talk to me right now, Jessica, and you're going to tell me if there are any other big events you neglected to mention."

I check my reflection in the mirror, but I see only fear and confusion in my eyes. There's still no sign of Jessica at all.

"Are you hiding from me?" I ask. "Is that it? Are you such a coward that you can't even face me and admit what you did?"

Leaning back in the seat, I realize that this has always been her way of getting a laugh. She probably kissed Nathan specifically because she wanted to shock me, although I suppose I should be glad that she kept things as *just* a kiss. Nathan apparently accepts that the whole thing doesn't mean I have a crush on him, but I still want to curl into a little ball and just forget that the rest of the world exists.

"Well?" I ask.

I wait, but I already know that she's not coming. In fact, Jessica has been A.W.O.L. for a while now, and I can't shake the feeling that she's hiding in our shared mind, trying to avoid dealing with the consequences of her actions. I still don't know a huge amount about the six months she spent in control, except that she bought a sports car and lost part of one of my fingers and kissed Nathan. Taking a deep breath, I remind myself that things might actually have been a whole lot worse, and that at least I came back to a job and a home and a relationship with Nathan that hasn't been completely destroyed.

"When you show your face again," I say out loud, convinced that on some level Jessica must be able to hear me, "we're going to talk. Do you understand? And believe me, I have got a *lot* to get off my chest!"

***

Once I've parked near Davis Drive, I sit staring out at the street ahead and once again tell myself that there's no need to stress about Jessica's actions. Everything seems to be more or less okay now, and I simply have to breathe a sigh of relief about the fact that no lasting damage was caused.

Plus, Nathan admitted that the kiss helped him consider the possibility of dating again, and that this in turn led him to accept a date with Sophia. In some ways, therefore, Jessica might even have helped him. Not that she would have been thinking about that, of course. Deep down, I know that – as usual – she was simply causing more chaos.

A moment later, spotting a car heading out of Davis Drive, I realize that my chance has arrived. I'm just about able to make out the Hoopers – all four of them – driving toward the edge of the village, and I'm fairly sure this means they must be going at least to the out-of-town shopping center, if not even further. I wait until their car has completely disappeared, and then I reach into my pocket and pull out the spare key to their house. I know I really shouldn't still have this, and that I absolutely shouldn't be doing what I'm about to do, but at the same time I figure that I have no choice.

Besides, my phone's in that house. Technically, I'm just retrieving stolen property.

***

As soon as I step into the hallway of the house on Davis Drive, I notice that the air seems strangely still and stuffy. I quickly bump the front door shut, and while I know that I might well be letting my imagination run wild, I can't shake the feeling that I can sense a presence here.

I listen to the silence for a moment, just to make sure that I'm truly alone, and then I reach into my pocket and pull out my spare phone. This is the phone I've kept around as a burner, just in case I ever get into more trouble, but now it's turning out to be surprisingly useful I bring up the number of my main phone and tap to dial, and then I wait. Sure enough, just a few seconds later, I hear my phone ringing somewhere nearby.

Upstairs.

As I start making my way up to the landing, following the sound of my ringtone, I can't help but sense that the air feels thicker somehow. There's definitely something here, a kind of presence that I can't believe anyone could ever miss, and by the time I get to the landing I'm absolutely convinced that this house contains a dark secret. Stopping for a moment, I listen as my phone stops ringing, but I can already tell that it appears to be in Lance Hooper's bedroom.

Stepping into that room, I glance out the window and immediately spot the exact area beyond the garden where I spent last night. I guess this room offers a perfect view of the spot where the gallows once stood, which might explain why this particular room seems to be the focal point of the negative energy in the house. At the same time, I know that I'm standing in almost the exact place where I saw Matt Hooper standing last night, and after a moment I turn and look toward the wardrobe at the other end of the room.

I tap my spare phone again, and sure enough I hear my other ringtone coming from somewhere inside the wardrobe. I can even see a faint flashing light through the crack in the doors, indicating that my phone is one one of the shelves.

Stepping closer, I find myself having to fight the urge to run. I've encountered evil before, but never quite to this degree. As I reach out and grab the handle, ready to pull the wardrobe door open and look for my phone, I realize that my hand is shaking. My phone is still ringing on the other side of the door, yet I hesitate for a moment as I try to find the courage to pull the door open and look inside.

And then, suddenly, my phone stops ringing and I realize that someone has answered.

I freeze, not daring to open the wardrobe door. I can hear a faint hissing sound coming from my spare phone, and when I press it against my ear I realize that someone or something is on the other end of the line.

"Hello?" I whisper, and I hear my voice coming from the phone in the wardrobe.

I wait, and now the hissing sound seems to be twisting slightly, as if it's becoming more of a pulsing rasping noise. I know there's a danger that I'm imagining things, but I can't shake the feeling that I can almost hear someone breathing into my other phone, as if there's a figure lurking in the wardrobe.

I'm still touching the handle, but I can't open

the door. Not yet. Not until I know what I might be about to see.

"Hello?" I say again. "Who are you?"

This time I hear a response; something lets out a faint, muffled groan, and now there can be no doubt that there's a presence hiding in this wardrobe. At first I think the groan sounds pained, but after a few seconds I realize that it seems to be shifting slightly, almost as if someone's laughing.

"Who are you?" I ask for a second time.

The laughter continues.

"What do you want with this family?" I continue, trying to hide the fear that even now is filling my voice. "Whatever you're after, you have to leave them alone. I can help you, but first you need to tell me who you are and why you're haunting this house? Are you someone who died on the gallows out there?"

The laughter hasn't even stopped, and I'm starting to feel as if this presence is trying to toy with me. I want to turn and run, but I know that won't get me anywhere so instead I take a moment to summon up a little more bravery and finally I do the only thing that makes sense.

As the laughter continues over my phone, I pull the wardrobe door open.

CHAPTER TWELVE

STARING INTO THE WARDROBE, I see no sign of anyone. As expected, my phone is resting on one of the shelves, but otherwise the scene seems remarkably normal.

I wait for a few more seconds, and now I realize that the laughter has faded. Reaching into the wardrobe, I pick up my phone and stare down at the screen; the call is still active, and I find myself wondering what kind of ghost would even know how to use a phone. Lance clearly hasn't begun to use the wardrobe for anything, and I can't help but wonder whether the entire Hooper family has come to understand that something's lurking in here.

Forcing myself to stay strong, I step forward and peer into the wardrobe, just to make sure that nothing's lurking in the shadows.

Suddenly an anguished snarl roars from my phone. Startled, I pull back and let the phone fall to the floor, but as I look down I see that the call has finally been cut. I look around the room, convinced that at any moment I'm about to spot a shadow figure, but there's no sign of anyone. I can tell that I'm being watched, however, and I know that I have to find some way to draw this presence out into the open.

"Don't you want to tell me how smart you are?" I ask finally. "You seem pretty stupid right now. Don't you want to brag and try to scare me?"

I was hoping that I could get the ghost to rise to a few insults, but I can already tell that this strategy isn't going to work. I guess the trick with the phone was an attempt to scare me away, and the ghost must be able to tell that its little plan hasn't worked. I've encountered plenty of ghosts in the past, of course, but this is the first one that seems to be trying to play a little prank on me. Does it know that I'm a threat, or does it simply see me as someone who's completely unimportant?

"I'm going to figure out who you are," I say firmly, "and when I do, I'm going to find a way to get rid of you. Don't you think you should save us both some time and just show yourself? There has to be something you want, and I'm perfectly willing to try to find it for you, but I'm going to need a few pointers."

I turn and look the other way.

"Or are you just going to keep playing games and hurting the people who live here? That doesn't seem like much of an existence. Are you trapped here? There's a way out, even if you need some help. I'm offering you that help, but the first step has to come from you."

I look over toward the window.

"If -"

Before I can get another word out, I spot a figure standing out by the edge of the forest. I feel my blood immediately start to run cold as I realize that this figure is a woman, wearing a white dress, and that she's staring straight at me. I tell myself that I might be wrong, but somehow even from this distance I can feel the woman's gaze burning into my eyes. I swear, it's as if she knows something, as if she's challenging me to go and ask her, and finally I realize that I have no choice.

Hurrying from the room, I race down the stairs, determined to get out there and talk to the woman. A couple of minutes later, however, I reach the forest's edge around the rear of the house and there's no sign of anyone. I call out, but all I hear in return is the rustle of leaves. Whoever that woman might have been – alive or dead – she's long gone now.

***

"The planning application has been approved," Horace murmurs as he reads from the letter he just opened, "so that removes the last major stumbling block. As far as I can tell, there's now nothing stopping us getting that lighthouse on the market."

As I stare out the window and watch the village green, I can't help thinking about that strange woman. I think I've developed a fairly good sense of when someone's alive and when they're a ghost, especially after everything that happened at Clute Cottage, and I'm certain I saw a ghost earlier today. There was something about the woman who was watching me, something about the intensity of her stare, that made me feel as if she wanted me to understand something. Of course, she was gone by the time I got outside, but I know that ghosts sometimes like to be a little cryptic. Was that woman trying to tell me something, or was she trying to warn me?

"It's going to be a new one for both of us," Horace continues. "The right person is going to pay big money for such a unique property, but ideally we'll have at least two bidders. That way, the price could soar. There are downsides, of course. The location might worry some people."

And then there's my phone. As I look down at the phone, which is charging now on my desk, I still don't understand how it managed to get into the house on Davis Drive. Even if someone happened to find me unconscious out there during the night, why would they take my phone and then leave me in the rain? It's not hard to come up with various outlandish theories, but none of them seem even remotely likely and I'm left with the feeling that I'm missing a big part of what's happening out there. I keep coming back to the strange figures in the night, and to the man whose silhouetted figure was left hanging from the gallows. How is that strange apparition connected to a wardrobe in a nearby house?

"Are you listening to me?"

Startled, I turn to Horace and I'm shocked to see Heidi standing right next to him. They're both staring at me, but in my befuddled state it takes me a few more seconds before I remember that Horace can't see Heidi at all.

"You were talking about the lighthouse," I stammer.

"We need to handle this property carefully," he replies. "Remember that guy who bought Payne Priory? The one who's turning it into a restaurant? What if we can get something similar set up for the lighthouse? It could be a really great little commercial location for someone who has a bit of imagination."

"I'm sure it could," I reply, sitting up a little straighter in my chair. "Did you look into the change of use documents?"

"I don't think there'd be a problem. The local council would support anything that brings investment to the area. It might have to wait until after the next election, when they'll be less worried about upsetting a load of nimby types, but that's not necessarily our problem. All we have to do is persuade someone with deep pockets that there's potential."

I open my mouth to reply to him, but at that moment I see that Heidi has reached down to touch the stapler on Horace's desk. Before I can say a word, I see that she's very slowly and very gently nudging it toward the edge, while keeping her eyes fixed on me.

"What do you think, Mercy?" Horace asks, evidently unaware of the stapler's movement. "Can we seize this opportunity?"

"Of course we can," I tell him, "and -"

Suddenly the stapler falls over the edge and drops down onto the carpet. Clearly confused, Horace leans over and looks down; he picks it up and sets it back on the desk, and then he turns to me.

"That's the second time something's fallen off my desk this week with no obvious explanation," he mutters, furrowing his brow. "If I didn't know better, I'd start to think this place is haunted."

"Absolutely," I reply, and now I can't help thinking that Heidi's stare is meant as a kind of warning. She's getting impatient, she wants me to solve her dilemma, and she's willing to start pushing. "Let's just all be very patient, though," I add, hoping that she'll get the message, "and remember that it never helps to rush. What we need now is to maintain our clear heads."

I wait, but Heidi's still glaring at me and I'm not sure that she's convinced.

"The lighthouse," Horace says firmly. "Let's just stay focused on the lighthouse." He looks back down at the letter. "I can just see it now," he continues. "Of course, the interior space isn't really an obvious location for a restaurant, or for a hotel, but someone who's good at this stuff would definitely be able to figure it out. That's half the charm."

As he continues to talk, I see that Heidi is now slowly sliding one of his pens toward the other side of the desk. She obviously wants some attention, but I wish she could just understand that sometimes the world of the living has to take priority over the world of the dead.

"Let's be sensible about this," I say, speaking to both Horace and Heidi at the same time. "Let's think before we do anything rash. We need to stay smart."

Heidi knocks the pen off the desk's side,

sending it down into the waste paper basket. Horace leans over and picks it out, and as he sets the pen back on the desk he seems doubly confused. At the same time, Heidi fades from view, although I know she thinks she's made her point.

"That's the craziest thing," Horace says, still staring at the pen. "I was joking earlier, but you don't think the office really *could* be haunted, do you? I mean, what kind of ghost would even bother?"

"I have no idea," I reply, fully aware that Heidi is probably still listening. "Maybe one that just needs to relax for a while?"

CHAPTER THIRTEEN

AS I MAKE MY way past the edge of the village green, heading toward the shop, I still feel extremely unsettled. My phone is fully charged now and in my pocket, but I keep going over the night's events in my mind and I can't work out how the phone got into that house.

I guess -

Suddenly a figure steps in front of me. Startled, I stop and see a familiar face staring back at me, although it takes a couple more seconds before I realize where I've seen this girl before.

"Hi, Ms. Willow," Ally Wistford says with a grin. "Do you remember me?"

"Ally," I stammer, genuinely shocked to be seeing her for the first time since we were in the house at Grove Weld. "How... how are you doing?"

"Just picking up a few things," she replies cheerily. "I couldn't believe it when I spotted you. How have you been since... well, since all that horrible stuff happened?"

"I'm fine," I reply, although I really don't feel that I'm in the right state to have this conversation at the moment. "Sorry, it's just a shock to see you."

"I was so sad about what happened to that Clarke woman," Ally continues. "I know there were times when she could seem pretty annoying, but when I heard she was dead... I guess it's just sad when a mother dies, you know? She had a husband and a kid, didn't she?"

"She did," I say cautiously.

"You were there when she died, right?"

"It's complicated," I tell her, choosing my words with great care. After all, I still don't know *exactly* what Ally might know and how much Jessica might have revealed. "I went out to her grave not long ago and left some flowers."

"I've been past the house a few times," she replies. "The one in Grove Weld. I don't think there's anything there anymore. There was a kind of presence there once, but whatever it was, it seems to have faded away to nothing. I guess we've got you to thank for that."

"I'm not sure I deserve any thanks," I tell her.

"And now here you are," she continues, as her smile grows even wider, "and you look so well! It's so typical of you to take flowers to the Clarke woman's grave. You brought some flowers to the hospital when I was in there, didn't you? You're so thoughtful, Ms. Willow. So many people in this world don't give a damn about anyone else, and it's really refreshing to meet someone who goes the extra mile." She pauses. "I suppose I just wanted to tell you that I admire you. Is that weird?"

"Not at all," I say cautiously, although my skeptical side is still waiting for some kind of punchline. "I think we all just need to be as helpful to one another as possible and -"

Before I can finish, I spot a figure lurking nearby. Looking over toward the shop, I see Martin Dunn watching us both; I instinctively offer a smile, but his expression doesn't change.

"Ally," he says finally, "we should go."

"Hey, Martin," I call out, and I can't help but notice that he seems much more withdrawn than before. "How are you doing?"

"Ally," he says again, not even acknowledging me. "We're going to miss the bus."

"He's such a sourpuss these days," Ally tells me, as she takes a couple of steps back. "It was good to bump into you again, Ms. Willow. I hope everything's going really well for you."

"And you," I reply as she turns and hurries

away.

Martin finally glances at me, but only for a second and it's clear that he's not exactly pleased to see me. I suppose he might know that I was involved in Jen's death, although this really doesn't feel like the right moment to go over and confront him about the details. Instead, I watch as he and Ally walk away across the green, past the spot where Horace's nephew Ashley is one again practicing his fighting moves. At some point I'm going to have to talk to Martin and find out what he knows, but right now I just need to focus on one problem at a time.

Reaching into my pocket, I take out my phone. I hadn't noticed before, but there are a few scratch marks around the side of the casing, and I swear those marks weren't there before.

***

"Oh, I wouldn't worry too much," Farrar says as I follow him across the dining room at Torfork Tower. "Don't get me wrong, I'm not dismissing your fears out of hand. It's just that the house on Davis Drive..."

His voice trails off as he reaches the large armchair in the corner. Reaching out to steady himself for a moment, he's clearly in some discomfort as he turns to me.

"It's just a fairly nondescript new-build," he continues finally. "It's boring to look at. I simply can't bring myself to believe that it's haunted."

"So ghosts only hang out in grand mansions and dilapidated old piles?" I ask, surprised by his attitude.

"That's not what I mean." He sighs. "Well, perhaps it is. I've done a little more research, Mercy, and as far as I can tell nobody has ever even died in that house. And unless I'm very much mistaken, someone dying tends to be prerequisite for there being a ghost."

"What about the land the house is on? You said it yourself, if -"

"If I encouraged you on this wild goose chase, then I'm sorry," he says, as he carefully takes a seat. "The incident you described with the gallows sounds rather unsettling, but it's simply a case of ghostly figures reenacting a traumatic incident. As for your phone, it's perfectly possible that you dropped it at some point and somebody found it."

"And then they took it inside and stuck it in the wardrobe?"

"If -"

"And then it answered itself?"

He hesitates, and I'm fairly sure that I've got him on that one. There's no way he can explain away so many unusual events.

"I have to prioritize," he says finally. "At

my age, I have to focus on the cases that I believe will be of most benefit to my research. Now, if you come with claims of a ghost at one of the big old houses around here, such as Harlham Hall or Mereford Mansion or Gower Grange or -"

"I've already done Gower Grange."

"You've *done* it?"

"I mean there was a ghost there and I fixed it," I tell him, and I have to admit that I'm feeling more than a little frustrated by his attitude. "Is there any chance that you could come to the house on Davis Drive one more time with me? I just want to rule some things out, and I have to admit that you're the one with more experience. There's a family living in that house and some kind of presence seems to be affecting them all. I'm worried that the longer they spend there, the worse things are going to get for them."

"I'm happy to look over any papers you might bring to me," he says, and now he sounds a little breathless, "and to help out in any other way, but I'm afraid I'm not available to go traipsing about in the Cornish countryside looking for minor ghosts that might not even exist." He hesitates, and I can tell that he's trying hard to disguise the fact that he's not feeling well. "You must understand the nature of my work," he adds. "Trifling little poltergeists don't really interest me a great deal."

"Are you okay?" I ask.

He looks up at me, and I can immediately see the answer in his eyes, even if I'm fairly sure that he's going to lie.

"I'm perfectly fine," he says, proving me right. "I didn't sleep well last night, that's all." He rubs the side of his belly. "To tell you the truth, I haven't slept well for a while now, but that's hardly a serious issue. I'm sure that eventually I'll get a good night, once my mind isn't racing with all these projects. And that, I'm sure you'll understand, is yet another reason why I can't possibly take on any additional work at the moment. I have to remain laser-focused. I'm close to making real progress, Mercy, and I can't let the momentum slip now. You can understand that, can't you?"

"Sure," I reply, although I'm struck by the realization that even in the short time I've known him, Farrar seems to have become noticeably sicker. "Just let me know if you need anything, okay?"

"You're not going to let this Davis Drive thing drop, are you? Why is that? Do you feel compelled to help every time you think there's a problem?"

"I'm not -"

"What are you trying to atone for, Mercy Willow?" he asks, fixing me with a friendly but determined stare, as if he's trying to read the answer in my eyes. "What did you do in the past that makes you so determined now to try to be a good person?"

CHAPTER FOURTEEN

"WHAT ARE YOU TRYING to atone for, Mercy Willow? What did you do in the past that makes you so determined now to try to be a good person?"

Those words are ringing in my head as I drive home. The hardest part is that Farrar was right – in some way – about me trying to make up for past sins, although he doesn't know that those sins are divided three ways. Then again, even when Annabelle and Jessica are discounted, I know that I haven't exactly been perfect. And as I pull into the driveway and switch the engine off, I realize that all my regrets are still so very close to the surface, and that they could come bubbling up again at any moment.

I sit for a moment in the darkness, wondering whether I could just walk away from

Davis Drive. Matt Hooper and his family are technically none of my responsibility, and I'm sure they can look after themselves. I'm hardly an expert when it comes to ghosts, at least not on the same level as Farrar, and there's a risk that I might just make things worse. I haven't really considered this possibility before, but can't I just forget about the place and just focus on being an ordinary estate agent? Why do I have to keep searching for trouble?

"You'd have an opinion on this, Jessica, wouldn't you?" I say out loud, hoping to goad her into making an appearance. "Perhaps I could use some hard truths right now."

I wait, but there's no sign of her. I don't know whether she's simply busy, or whether she's punishing me, but I have to admit that I'm actually starting to miss her. That's probably the craziest admission of my life, but – for better or for worse – Jessica is my oldest and closest friend. We understand each other, we share a mostly common aim, and we've helped each other out whenever Annabelle has tried to break back through. I don't know where Jessica is right now, I can only assume that she's battling away somewhere deep inside our shared mind, but I wish she could take a break for just a few minutes and pop out to give me some advice.

Then again, I should probably learn to get by without her.

"Okay, then," I mutter, as I start climbing out of the car. "Time to get on with things."

***

There's someone else I miss, too, even though I feel silly for saying this. As I stand in my kitchen and listen to the silence around, I actually find myself wondering whether I gave Miss Chloe up a little too early. I didn't have her for long, but I already miss the sound of her paws following me around wherever I go.

"You're better off with Nathan and Lily," I say under my breath as I head to the counter and grab the kettle. "They can give you way more -"

Suddenly I freeze as I hear a brief clicking sound coming from somewhere over my shoulder. I hesitate, still holding the kettle, and after a moment I glance at the glass on the front of the microwave. This glass affords me a decent reflected view of the rest of the kitchen, and so far I don't see any sign of anyone or anything nearby. Once I'm sure that the coast is clear, I turn and take a look for myself, and I breathe a sigh of relief as I find that I'm definitely alone.

"Don't get jumpy," I murmur, before heading to the sink and filling the kettle. "You really can't afford to lose your mind."

Once I've set the kettle on to boil, I make

my way over to the dining table. As I get there, however, I notice that something seems different. My laptop has been left with the lid open, which is strange since I *always* close it right before I leave each day. I tap to wake it up, and I feel an instant rush of fear as I see a message on the screen warning me that I've made too many failed attempts to enter my password.

Except... I didn't do that.

Slowly, I look around the room, and now I'm genuinely worried that there might be someone else here. I listen for even the slightest hint of a sound, although the continued silence doesn't exactly make me feel a huge amount better. In fact, I can't help but worry that someone might be watching me right now, peering at me from the shadows. I've encountered the odd ghost here since I moved in, but at this particular moment I'm more worried about an intruder who's very much alive. After all, why would a ghost be trying to get into my laptop?

"If there's someone here," I say cautiously, "you need to leave right now, okay? I have a knife and I know how to defend myself."

Realizing that I actually *don't* have a knife, I hurry back to the kitchen and start rooting through one of the drawers. Finding a large carving knife, I turn and brandish it in the air so that any would-be attacker will be able to see the blade.

"I'm not kidding!" I continue. "You've got ten seconds to get the hell out of here before I call the police."

The police? There's no way I can do that. On top of all the other problems I might encounter, there's the small matter of that Reid guy who – as far as I know – remains extremely suspicious of me. There are plenty of other reasons why I really shouldn't invite the police into my life, but as I keep my back against the cupboards and slowly inch toward the hallway I figure that I at least need to act tough and make some threats.

"I'm not a pushover," I say firmly. "I've had to defend myself in tougher situations than this, so don't think that I'm some meek little thing who'll pull away at the first sign of trouble. I know what I'm doing."

I wait, but the silence continues and now I'm trying to work out whether there's any way I might have been mistaken. Sure, I always close my laptop before I head out, but I suppose it's possible that for once I was distracted; as for the password issue, I really don't know how that could have happened but there might be some kind of software glitch. I really want to calm down and just try to get a relaxing night, and with each passing second I feel myself starting to accept that I might have been wrong, until finally I start to lower the knife.

Suddenly the doorbell rings behind me,

almost making my leap out of my skin. I turn and look at the door, and then I step over to the peephole and peer out.

Nothing.

No-one.

I hesitate, and then I pull the door open and look out at the darkness. There's still no sign of whoever rang the bell, although I suppose some local kids might be playing a game. I feel a strong chill in the air, but after a moment I turn to head back inside.

"Ms. Willow?"

Letting out a shocked gasp, I turn and find to my surprise that Diane Hooper is standing outside. I swear she wasn't there a moment ago, but she's certainly there now and she's fixing me with a very calm but also very determined stare.

"Hi," I say cautiously, trying to hide the fact that I almost screamed with shock. "I'm sorry, I heard the doorbell go but..."

My voice trails off as I try to work out exactly what she wants. I wait, hoping that she'll start talking, but she seems content to merely stare at me and after a moment I start to realize that she looks even thinner and paler than before. I still don't know exactly what's going on at the house on Davis Drive, but it's clearly taking a toll on this woman's well-being and I think that perhaps I need to offer her some help.

"Do you want to come in?" I ask, before stepping aside and gesturing for her to enter. "I won't bite, I promise."

Again I wait, and again she shows no obvious reaction. I'm really struggling here, and I'm starting to wonder whether she really knows why she's here.

"It's okay," I continue, hoping to seem as friendly as possible. "I won't judge you, and anything you tell me will be kept in the strictest confidence."

"There's nothing I want to tell you," she replies, keeping her eyes fixed on me. "It's my husband."

"Your husband?"

"He's the one who wants to talk to you."

"Okay," I say, still trying to figure all of this out, "then -"

Before I can finish, I hear a faint shuffling sound over my shoulder. I start to turn, but at that moment a hand reaches around and clamps a wet cloth firmly over my mouth and nose. I try to pull away, but another arm pulls me tight and Diane rushes forward to grab my arms. No matter how hard I struggle, I'm powerless to resist as I feel some kind of noxious substance filling my nostrils, and a fraction of a second later I realize that I'm losing consciousness.

"Lower her down," I hear a man's voice

saying, sounding further and further away with each passing second as I start to pass out. "I've got her. Get the car."

CHAPTER FIFTEEN

"HEY."

Opening my eyes, I find myself standing in a blindingly bright white room. I blink a few times, trying to get used to the light, and then I see that Jessica is sitting on the edge of a desk over at the room's far end. At least, I *think* it's the far end, but I can't be sure since the walls seem so very far away.

"Relax," Jessica continues, swinging her legs a little, "there's nothing to worry about. You've just been drugged and knocked out, that's all."

"What are you talking about?" I ask, trying not to panic.

"The question is, am I really here?" she adds. "Is this really me, keeping you company while you're out for the count, or am I a figment of your imagination? What do you think, Mercy? If you really had to place a bet, if you had to put some money down, which of those two options would you go for?"

"I don't know what you mean," I reply, as I start to remember the cold, wet cloth against my face. I instinctively reach up, but there's nothing there now. Still, I swear I felt something burning my nostrils, as if I was forced to breathe in something that knocked me out cold. "I don't know what's happening."

"You're in your own mind," she says with a heavy sigh. "The only question is, am I really here right now or am I some kind of psychological comfort blanket?"

"How do I wake up?"

"You need to wait for the drugs to wear off. That's what I think, anyway. You might be surprised to learn that I'm no expert when it comes to kidnapping people." She pauses, and then she lets out a faint chuckle. "Actually, to be honest, that *is* a bit of a surprise, isn't it? You'd think I would have had a go at that by now."

"I want to wake up," I stammer, turning and looking the other way but only seeing more empty white space. I'm not even sure this room still has walls. "Where's my body right now?"

"You're out like a light. If I had to guess, I'd say you're probably in the back of a car, being transported somewhere."

I turn to her again.

"Don't panic, though," she adds with a grin. "Hey, what if these people are just organizing a surprise party for you?"

"Help me wake up."

"I can't."

She gets to her feet and starts walking toward me. There's something strangely confident about the way she's carrying herself, as if she thinks she has the upper hand over me. To be fair, right now that's probably a fair assumption.

"I *really* can't help you get out of this dream," she adds, before stopping and putting a hand on my shoulder, "but this little interlude might yet serve a useful purpose. There's something you've been ignoring, Mercy, and it shouldn't take a figment of your imagination for you to figure out what that might be. It's actually something extremely obvious, although you really need to try to focus on something that happened a while ago."

"I don't -"

"Don't tell me you don't understand," she says firmly, her mood changing in an instant. Now she seems angry. "Don't try that passive crap when I'm trying to explain things." She grabs my other shoulder and forces me to turn around. "You must know that something's wrong."

Before I can answer, I see that there's a door facing me. I swear that door wasn't there a moment ago, but it's there now and something about its faded, damaged wooden surface seems strangely familiar. I feel as if I've seen this door before, but I have no idea where or when. All I know is that I can feel a sense of genuine dread slowly creeping up through my chest, threatening to explode and fill me with absolute terror. I know that I need to stay calm if I'm going to have any hope of getting out of here, but somehow my body seems to be reacting independently.

"Take a peek," Jessica whispers in my ear.

"No."

"No? Why not?"

"What's in there?"

"You know *exactly* what's in there," she replies, giving my shoulder a little extra squeeze. "That's the problem, but you need to actually see it with your own two eyes. I need you to face the truth, Mercy. I need you to be honest about the mess we're in right now." She squeezes even harder, as if she's extra determined to make sure that I understand whatever nonsense she's going on about. "You know that something's wrong," she adds, lowering her voice slightly. "You've known for a while. You can't hide from the truth forever. And this particular truth has been hiding in plain sight for a long time now. You just made one very bad assumption."

I open my mouth to reply, but somehow the

words catch in the back of my throat. I want to scream at her, to tell her that she's wrong, but deep down I know she's telling the truth.

Finally, stepping forward, I reach for the handle. Every fiber in my body is trying to pull back, but I manage to push through the fear; taking hold of the handle, I give it a turn and pull the door open, revealing nothing but darkness on the other side. Just as I'm about to point this out, however, I realize that I can hear a faint gasping sound.

"What *is* that?" I ask, before turning to see that Jessica has vanished. "Jessica, where are you?"

Realizing that she's gone, I look back into darkness, just as I start to hear a series of anguished groans. Before I can react, a bloodied and naked figure crawls into view, barely managing to drag itself across the floor. The figure stops and looks up at me, and behind the terrified eyes and bloodied, matted hair I realize that I recognize her.

"Jessica?" I stammer. "What -"

"Run!" she screams. "You've made a terrible mistake! You have to -"

***

"Run!" I gasp, suddenly opening my eyes and sitting up. "What -"

I freeze. Blinking wildly, I already know that I've just escaped from some kind of dream. I remember seeing Jessica on the floor, and hearing her voice screaming at me, but already the dream is starting to fade and I realize that I'm on my side on a dusty concrete floor. I feel strangely groggy, and as I start to sit up I quickly find that the world seems to be spinning around me. I pull back and lean against the wall, and now I tell myself that I simply have to wait and try to get my head together.

After a few more seconds, I spot a set of shelves on the far side of the room. There are various boxes on the shelves, and a couple of bikes have been left propped against one of the walls. This place feels strangely familiar, but also decidedly mundane, and I'm certain that I've been here before. I lean forward, and at that moment I realize that my hands are tied together. Somehow my brain wasn't switched on when I first woke up, and it's only now that I'm noticing that my feet are bound too, and that there's a tight section of tape over my mouth.

I try to call out, but all I manage is a muffled groan. Trying not to panic, I lean back against the wall before carefully getting to my feet. With my ankles tied together, I know there's no way I'll be able to get very far, but as I look around I realize that I'm in some sort of basement.

"There's nothing I want to tell you," I hear a female voice saying. "It's my husband."

"Lower her down," a man's voice replies.

"I've got her. Get the car."

The Hoopers. In this moment, I suddenly remember that Diane Hooper came to my door, and that I was aware of someone lurking nearby. I have a vague memory that I felt something cold and wet getting pressed against my face, and finally I understand that I must have been drugged. I look around, and I'm slowly starting to understand where I've seen this room before. I came down here when I was showing people around the house on Davis Drive, which means that I've been captured and tied up here in the basement.

I try to tell myself that I have to stay calm, but I instinctively start pulling on the ropes and I can already feel a sense of panic starting to spread throughout my body.

"Help me!" I try to scream, although I'm unable to make much noise at all. "Somebody get me out of here!"

CHAPTER SIXTEEN

A COUPLE OF HOURS later – or perhaps more, since I really have no sense of time down here – I slam myself against the door yet again. I've been making no progress so far, but I can't just sit around in this basement and wait for a miracle.

Stepping back, I pause for a moment as I try to reassess my priorities. Turning, I spot the small rectangular window at the top of the far wall. This window looks out onto a view that's almost completely obscured by grass, and I'm not even sure that I could fit through, but I'm starting to think that my earlier plan might be worth revisiting. I assumed that the window would be inaccessible, and that with my hands and feet bound I'd never be able to climb up there and escape. Now that the door is proving useless, however, I'm starting to wonder whether I should perhaps give the window a proper try.

I make my way over. Already, I can see that the window looks fairly secure, although it's also dirty and old. I think it's definitely worth a shot, but a moment later – just as I stand on tip-toes to get a better look – I hear footsteps making their way down a nearby set of stairs. Reaching up, I use my shoulder to rub at the tape over my mouth and finally I manage to push it aside.

I turn just as a key slides into a lock, and a moment later the door swings open to reveal Matt Hooper.

"Why am I here?" I stammer, unable to hide a sense of fear. "Why did you bring me here?"

He hesitates, before stepping forward and leaning down. I watch as he sets a tray of food on the floor, along with a glass of water, and then he turns and heads back to the door.

"Wait!" I call out, hurrying after him as fast as I can. "You can't do this! People are going to notice that I'm missing!"

He turns to me, and as I come to a halt I see the anger and hatred in his eyes. I remember the very first time I met this man, on a sunny morning when he and his wife arrived to take their first look around this house; he was friendly and actually quite charming, but now he almost seems like an entirely different person.

"Talk to me," I continue, as I try once again to pull on the ropes around my wrists. "I'm sure we can work this out if we just talk it all through."

"There's nothing to talk about," he says calmly.

"I think there's *plenty* to talk about," I tell him. "Why have you tied me up? Why did you kidnap me?"

I wait, but he says nothing; he seems irritated by my questions, although if that's the case I don't understand why he doesn't simply walk away.

"Talk to me, Matt," I continue, desperately trying to buy some time and get as much information out of him as possible. "I can help but you first you have to talk to me."

"It doesn't matter what we say," he replies. "None of it matters. All that matters is my family's happiness, and in this house there's only one way to guarantee that."

"But -"

"This house that *you* sold us, by the way," he adds, interrupting me. "It's your fault that we're in this mess, Ms. Willow. If you'd been a little more careful and not allowed us to end up in this position, we could be happily living somewhere else right now. We'd never have had to know about the things that are going on in this house, but you let us come waltzing right into the jaws of danger. To be honest,

Ms. Willow, I think it's completely appropriate that you should be the one we offer up."

"Offer up?"

"Sit tight," he adds, stepping past the door. "It won't be long now. As soon as night falls, he'll be ready for you."

"Who?" I ask, but at that moment he swings the door shut. "Wait! Who are you talking about?"

Shuffling forward, I throw myself against the door. I can already hear the key turning in the lock again, but I know I can't let Matt Hooper simply walk away.

"I have to know!" I yell, even as I hear him heading back up the stairs. "Who's making you do this? Matt, you have to talk to me! Why are you doing this to me?"

***

Some more flecks of pain fall away from the small window, but the actual wooden frame remains stubbornly in place. Balancing on a tin of paint, I've just about managed to reach up high enough, although so far my attempts to break the glass have come to nothing. I'm trying to force the wood, but so far I'm not having much luck with that either.

Although the glass is absolutely filthy, I can just about see that the sky outside is starting to darken again, which can only mean one thing. Night is starting to fall, and I'm getting closer and closer to whatever Matt Hooper is planning.

Suddenly a shadow moves on the other side of the window. I almost fall back, but I force myself to stay strong and a moment later a figure kneels on the grass outside and peers in at me.

"Katie?" I whisper, before tapping on the glass furiously. "Katie, help! You have to call someone!"

I wait, but through the dirty glass I can just about make out her eyes. She's staring at me with a somewhat blank expression, and already I'm worried that she might be part of whatever her parents are planning. At the same time, she's just a child, and I tell myself that there has to be some way to get through to her.

"Katie," I continue, "can you do something for me? Can you go and tell someone that I'm here?"

Again I wait, but I'm not even sure that she's paying attention to a word I just said. I'm certain that she must be too young to have been corrupted, yet at the same time I'm troubled by her strangely calm demeanor.

"Katie, this is really important," I continue, "if -"

Before I can finish, a second figure appears. I watch as Katie's brother Lance kneels on the grass next to her, and now they're both staring in at me.

"Guys, hey," I add, trying to sound as friendly as possible, "this must seem pretty odd to you, huh? Did your parents tell you that I'm down here? It's okay, no-one's going to be mad at you, but I have a really important job that I need you to do for me. Do you know where Torfork Tower is?"

The two kids look at one another for a moment. When they turn back to me, they seem a little hesitant, but Lance finally nods.

"That's great," I continue. "I need you to go to Torfork Tower and find a man named Clement Farrar who lives there. He might seem a little grumpy at first, but you have to tell him that I've been kidnapped and that I'm being kept here. He'll know what to do next. I really don't want to get the police involved, and I'm convinced that he'll only call them if it's absolutely necessary. But you have to hurry, okay? Can you do that for me?"

They stare at me, and I can't help but notice that they're not exactly leaping into action.

"Please?" I add.

"You're funny," Lance says suddenly, tilting his head. "Dad said you might try something like this. He told us that you wouldn't really understand."

"He told us not to listen to you too much," Katie adds. "He told us that you're against what we're doing and that you want us to stay trapped here like this forever."

"He told us," Lance continues, "that if we listen to you, we'll be trapped here forever and that we'll never be able to get away. But if we *don't* listen to you, then we have a chance. All we have to do is give the bad man what he wants, and then he might take pity on us and leave us alone."

"What are you talking about?" I ask, trying desperately to figure out what they mean. "What bad man?"

"He said you'd try to confuse us," Katie replies, before getting to her feet. "I'm sorry, I feel really mean, but we have to do what Daddy tells us to do. Daddy's always right. About everything. If we don't listen to Daddy..."

Her voice trails off, and a moment later Lance also stands up.

"Hey, wait!" I call out as they start walking away. "I need you to come back! You can't just leave me down here! Who were you talking about just now? Who are you trying to get away from?"

Realizing that they're not coming back, I hesitate for a moment as I try to figure out what to try next. I'm fairly sure that there's no way I'll manage to break through that reinforced window, and the ropes around my wrists and ankles are too tight to pull aside. Finally, as I continue to look up at the window and see the fading light outside, I tell myself that I only have one chance.

"Help!" I shout, hoping desperately that

someone in one of the other houses might hear me. "I'm down here! Somebody help me!"

CHAPTER SEVENTEEN

THE KEY TURNS IN the lock, and a moment later the door swings open to reveal a figure silhouetted against the stairs. To my surprise, as I sit on the floor and wait for my fate, I see that this figure isn't Matt Hooper.

"Hello," Diane says, and I can hear the fear in her voice. "Matt wants... I've been sent to fetch you."

Night has well and truly fallen, and I've been expecting company for a while. I still have no idea what the Hoopers are planning to do with me, but I've managed to piece together a few possibilitics. The children referred to a 'bad man', and I'm fairly sure that this must be the entity that's taken up residence in one of the bedrooms. Quite what this entity wants is unclear, but it's clearly a malignant force that has – to varying degrees – managed to exert control over the entire family.

"Get up," Diane says firmly.

"Why?" I ask.

"Don't make this any more difficult than it already is. We heard you shouting for help earlier. The only reason Matt didn't come down and discipline you is that he knew nobody would be able to hear you. There's no way you can run away, so really, you just have to come with me."

"I don't feel much like being cooperative," I tell her.

"If you just -"

"And I don't like being locked up," I add, cutting her off. "Believe me, this isn't the first time it's happened and it's something I was really hoping I'd never have to relive." I wait for an answer, but I can tell that she seems less certain than her husband, less sure that this is the right thing to do.

I can exploit that doubt.

"There's a better way of dealing with the problem," I continue, as I slowly struggle to my feet. My hands and feet are still bound, despite my best efforts to pull them free, and I'm fully aware that there's no way I can fight my way to freedom. Instead, I'm going to have to try to talk my way out of trouble. "Diane, I've said this before but I'm going to say it again, I can help you. You and Matt came to me originally, remember? You wanted me to do something, and I'm offering to figure this all out for you. But we have to work together."

"You're stalling," she replies. "Matt's waiting upstairs. We have to go."

"Tell me what -"

"We're not bad people," she continues, and now she seems to be on the verge of tears. "Really, we're not. We're just in a bad situation, and Matt and I... we have to look after our children. It doesn't even matter what happens to us, but we have to do whatever it takes to keep Lance and Katie safe, even if that means..."

Her voice trails off, and I'm starting to realize that I'm unlikely to get much more information out of her. For better or for worse, Matt's clearly the one who's in charge and that means I have to talk to him directly.

***

A few minutes later, once Diane has led me upstairs – with my feet free from the ropes but my hands every much still bound, like the prisoner that I am – I stop in another doorway and look through into the front room. Matt's sitting at the table, looking through some papers, and I'm fairly sure that he deliberately ignores me for a few seconds before finally looking up.

"Ms. Willow," he says with a faint smile.

"Or can I call you Mercy?"

"How about you call me free?"

"Please, sit down."

"Or I could just scream," I point out. "From here, people might even be able to hear me."

"They might, or they might not," he replies, "but you'd be taking quite a big risk. I'm willing to discuss the situation with you, but only if you cooperate."

Before I have a chance to reply, I feel hot breath against the back of my neck. Turning, I see that Diane is right behind me, and I quickly realize that I have no choice here. I step forward, entering the room, and I can't help but notice that Matt and his wife seem very clinical right now, as if they've been planning this whole operation for a while. The house feels more like a jail than a home, and the heavy atmosphere I previously detected upstairs now seems to permeate every room.

"You took my phone," I say finally.

"No, that wasn't me."

"Then -"

"There are forces at work here," he continues. " Forces that defy easy understanding. The point is that your phone was brought in here by something that's curious. By something that wants you."

"You're not making any sense," I say as I glance around, hoping to spot something I can use as a weapon.

"Kidnapping you was nothing personal," Matt explains. "The truth is, when we moved into this house, we were a happy family. Pretty soon, though, we noticed that something was very wrong with Lance's room. He noticed it first, but the change in his personality was remarkable and soon we were all affected to one degree or another. Whatever's in there, it's spreading out and it's taking control, but the good news is that we've figured out what it wants. And if we can give it what it wants, there's a good chance that it'll leave us alone."

"You're talking about a ghost."

"Call it whatever you want to call it," he replies, "but my responsibility is to protect my family."

"There are different ways of going about that," I tell him.

"I've chosen the easiest option," he continues. "You can't blame me for that. I just want this thing to leave us alone, and for that to happen we need to satisfy its hunger. And that's the whole point here, Mercy. This presence isn't just hungry, it's *starving*, and you must know that starving creatures tend to get desperate."

"Has it promised you something?"

"We're going to give him what he wants tonight."

"Who are you talking about?"

"The man," he replies matter-of-factly, as if this answer is the most natural response in the world. "He's been dead for a long time, that much I'm sure of, and he's been testing his newfound powers very slowly. As far as I can tell, this land was vacant until a few decades ago, but the construction of these houses has worked to focus his mind. I'm not about to dig down into the foundations, Mercy, but my bet is that his body is down there somewhere far beneath the house. I suppose in a horror movie we'd dig him up and bless his bones, something like that, and he'd finally be at peace. But short of ripping the house down, that's not an option, so we're going to have to go with the next best option."

"Which is?"

"Which is feeding him. Satisfying him. Giving him what he wants so that he backs off."

"Haven't you forgotten something?" I ask. "This entity, whatever or whoever he is, will just get hungry again."

"Oh, I know that," he tells me, "but we intend to be long gone from here by then. We'll sell up and get away, and then the entity can be a problem for the next owners. The point is, I'm a father and a husband and I refuse to let anything hurt my family."

I take a couple of steps toward him. He seems very firm and very sure of himself, but I'm convinced that there has to be some way to break through this certainty and get him to rethink this whole approach.

"So what are you going to do?" I ask. "Sacrifice me? Throw me to the wolves?"

I wait for an answer, and to be honest each passing second makes me worry that I'm a little closer to the truth than I'd imagined.

"It's not quite like that," he explains. "There are things out there in the darkness, Mercy. These things shouldn't exist, but they do, and they're part of this whole mess. They used to help him, and they still want to do that. I guess sometimes loyalty never truly dies."

"I still don't know what you're talking about," I tell him.

"I'm talking about this man," he replies, before taking a moment to sort through some of the papers. Finally he holds up a photocopy of an old painting, rendered in black-and-white and showing a stern-looking man. "I'm talking about Lawrence Radcliffe."

"Never heard of him," I say, even as I feel a shudder run through my bones.

"You should have done," Matt says firmly. "Many years ago, Lawrence Radcliffe was the chief executioner for this whole region, particularly in the Candleward area." He sets the picture down and slides it toward me. "And tonight, for the first time in a few hundred years, he's going to kill again."

CHAPTER EIGHTEEN

THREE HUNDRED YEARS EARLIER, Lawrence Radcliffe stood on a hill at the edge of Candleward and stared up at the magnificent new scaffold that had been erected by his man.

"Will this do, Sir?" one of the men asked as he made his way over.

"I want every man, woman and child in this village to see the consequences of law-breaking," Radcliffe replied, turning to him. He paused, looking the man up and down and making no attempt to hide his disdain for the fellow's dirty clothing. "I don't care if I have to hang a hundred wretches – or a thousand, even – but I will ensure that no more smuggling takes place in this part of the land."

"Very good, Sir," the man replied.

"Do your bit," Radcliffe continued. "Spread the word. I know you spend your evenings in those terrible public houses in the village. Tell everyone you meet that Candleward is now going to obey the rule of law."

Over the next few years, Radcliffe followed through on his threats. Smuggler after smuggler found himself hauled up the hill and hung from the gallows, and Radcliffe displayed great pleasure every time he heard the cracking sound of a breaking neck. Women begged for their husbands to be spared, children sobbed at the thought of losing their fathers, but for Radcliffe this only proved that his approach was working. Gradually the smugglers moved on, and many of the locals – while having not approved of Radcliffe's methods – had to admit that he'd cleaned the area up.

And yet, as the smuggling problem faded away, Radcliffe realized that he missed the thrill of killing so many miscreants. He began to loiter near the gallows, looking up at the noose and wondering when – or whether – he might get to kill again. By this point he was almost addicted to the sight of a body swinging from the rope, and to the sense of importance he gained from carrying out a duty that honored both the king and the Lord. No matter how hard he tried to convince himself that he'd simply done a good job, he instead began to wonder whether in fact the smuggling industry had merely adapted to his presence and was now operating fully out of sight.

Soon Radcliffe became a familiar presence in the village, constantly knocking on doors at all hours of the day and night, demanding to be let inside so that he could conduct a search. He had a warrant, that much was certain, although many believed that he was vastly overstepping the mark and abusing his authority. He regularly charged from house to house, sometimes checking the same property twice or even three times on a single night, and the less contraband he found, the more certain he felt that it was all being hidden from him. He swore revenge on anyone he caught, even going so far as to insist that their families would hang as well, but all his searches left him empty-handed.

Finally he could bear such madness no longer.

If the smugglers were truly hiding their wares, that meant that they had to be using some kind of special power, and this in turn led Radcliffe to consider the possibility of supernatural involvement. Having long believed that witches were a real force, he now developed a complex theory that he believed explained his failures: he began to explain to his associates that the local smugglers had evidently employed the help of witches to confound and confuse anyone with a pure heart, and he insisted that his authority stretched to a new aim: the detection and prosecution of any witches found in the Candleward area.

"He's lost his mind," one man muttered in the public house on a cold winter evening. "He's started talking to himself."

"As long as he's here on the king's authority," a fellow drinker replied, "there's nothing we can do about him. Apart from trying to ignore him, that is."

"How can we ignore him if he keeps barging into our homes?" a third man asked. "If you ask me, Lawrence Radcliffe seems almost possessed."

Suspicion grew, and this only fueled Radcliffe's suspicions further. Whereas previously he'd been convinced that the locals were hiding smugglers and witches, now he came up with his craziest theory yet: he decided that *all* the inhabitants of Candleward were directly involved in such illicit activity, and that they must all be conspiring behind his back. He took to watching the locals from a distance, making constant notes about their behavior and coming up with increasingly convoluted theories to explain their behavior. More than anything, he was starting to develop plans for dealing with the lawlessness he felt certain was happening under his nose.

And then one day, by chance, he happened to notice a young boy named John Philpott heading out of the village.

Convinced that the boy – who was only eight or nine years old – must be part of the plot, Radcliffe followed him. Once they were away from everyone else, Radcliffe approached the boy and grabbed him by the arm, demanding to know the details of his plans. The boy protested that he knew nothing, that he was simply going to gather samphire, but Radcliffe became increasingly irate and began to push the boy around. The more John denied that he was involved in any kind of plot, the more Radcliffe felt his fury growing, until finally he picked up a rock and threatened to bash the boy's brains out.

"Tell me everything!" he snarled as the boy began to cry with fear. "Tell me now, or I'll send you straight to Hell!"

The boy once again denied any knowledge, and this was enough to push Radcliffe over the edge. He brought the rock crashing down against the side of the boy's head, crushing his skull and killing him instantly.

Shocked by his own actions, Radcliffe hesitated for a moment. He'd never intended to actually hurt the boy; instead he'd merely wanted to grill him for information, and to perhaps send him home with a clip around the ear and a warning for the other conspirators. Now, however, he knew that he'd become one of the very criminals he'd spent his life trying to track down, although after a few seconds he began to come up with another explanation. The boy had been engaged in nefarious activity, in which case Radcliffe reasoned that perhaps he'd done the right thing after all. He looked around, to make sure that nobody was nearby, and then he crouched down and rolled the boy over.

"I'm sorry that it has come to this," he murmured as he began to search the boy's pockets. "It's not my fault, though. You should never have let yourself get lured into such treachery and -"

Stopping suddenly, he felt a small hard packet in one of the pockets. Pulling it out, he swiftly saw that it was a pouch containing a number of silver coins. As he turned the pouch around, he saw that it was marked with a strange logo, seemingly one depicting a pair of horns floating above a single eye. Radcliffe had never before seen such a strange image, but he was immediately struck by a sense of something demonic. He felt a slow sense of fear starting to spread through his body, and within seconds he'd begun to conjure up thoughts of mysterious ceremonies being conducted just out of his line of vision.

He looked around again, and now he found himself wondering whether he'd been naive. Whereas previously he'd assumed that the wrongdoers were in the minority, now he worried that the entire village might be against him.

"May the Lord have mercy on my soul," he whispered as he looked back down at the pouch, before glancing once again at the blood on the side of the side of the boy's head. "When a good man confronts this much evil, there is only one thing for him to do. He must fight."

Still holding the pouch, he got to his feet. He told himself that he needed time to think, that he had to be careful so as to avoid arousing suspicion, yet at the same time he worried that the Lord might judge him for acting too slowly. Every second was a second missed, and he felt a sharp pain in the back of his head as he watched the sky briefly filling with a reddish shade.

"I was right to kill this lad," he stammered, trying to push down any sense of fear or regret or shame. "I'm a man of the law, and of the Lord as well, and I simply *must* act swiftly."

He felt frozen in place, as if the magnitude of his discovery was too great, but finally he turned and began to head back to the village. More than anything, he knew now that he'd been right all along, and that he had a duty to rid all of Candleward of the foulest evil imaginable.

CHAPTER NINETEEN

Today...

"SO THIS RADCLIFFE GUY," I say cautiously, still staring at the image on the desk, "was some kind of local executioner who went crazy. And now he's living in your wardrobe and..."

My voice trails off as I try once more to make sense of this madness. I just about managed to follow the convoluted tale that Matt told me, although I'm still struggling to work out how it relates to the present day. Sure, the ghost of Lawrence Radcliffe might very well be lurking in this house, but some of the details of this story seem a little too specific.

"You don't *have* to understand," Matt tells me.

I look over at him, just as he gets to his feet.

"None of us do," he continues. "All we have to do is give that thing what it wants. And in this case, what it wants is to feed again. On blood."

"Like some kind of sacrifice?" I ask.

"It's not a sacrifice," he replies. "It's more that... this thing needs death, and it's going to get what it needs one way or another. And I can't let it hurt anyone in my family, which means that I have to find someone else. You've been poking around, and I'm afraid you kind of pushed yourself into consideration. Then I found your phone in here and _"

"My phone was outside," I tell him. "Didn't you bring it in here?"

"Perhaps the entity wanted you all along," he continues. "Whatever, the details don't really matter. What matters is that after tonight, my family will be free. I'm certain that the entity will rest after it's eaten, and that'll give us time to sell this place and move away. That'll be tough, but we've come to realize that it's the only option. You have to understand that I can't let anything bad happen to my children."

"So how are you planning to do it?" I ask, playing for time as I try to figure out how to get out of here.

"Sometimes a scaffold appears outside," he explains. "Just beyond the garden. I don't really know how that process works, but I've seen it plenty of times. Once it returns, I have a feeling that Lawrence Radcliffe himself will take over and do the rest of the job."

"You're going to let him hang me?"

"I'm going to save my family."

He steps closer. I want to turn and run, but I know Diane's loitering out in the corridor and I have no doubt that she's got some way of stopping me. I need to be smarter, although with each passing second I'm getting more and more worried about the glint in Matt's eyes. If I didn't know better, I swear I'd think that he's actually enjoying all of this.

"Thank you for not screaming, by the way," he continues. "I could stop you, of course, but you've saved us both a lot of trouble."

"I think I should conserve my energy," I tell him.

"There's no point wasting any more time," he adds, reaching out and putting a hand on the side of my arm. "It's time."

"You don't -"

"I see it," he says, and I suddenly realize that he's looking past me. "It's out there, and it's ready."

Turning, I see nothing but the window. After a moment, however, I step over and peer out into the darkness. My eyes take a few seconds to adjust, but finally I feel a thud of terror in my chest as I spot a set of gallows standing in the darkness. This is the same structure that I saw once before, the same structure that felt so solid and so real, and now it's out there waiting for me.

"I have to save my wife and children," Matt says, stepping up behind me and taking hold of my arm again. "Please try to understand that. At heart, I'm a family man."

***

A couple of minutes later, as I'm led out through the gate at the end of the garden and toward the foot of the grassy slope, I look up once again at the gallows and I realize that this might actually be a good time to scream.

Sure, screaming feels cliched and counter-productive, but at least I might be able to attract some attention. I keep telling myself that I can talk my way out of this, or that I'll figure out some kind of loophole, but already I'm starting to make my way up the slope and I can feel the air getting colder. I almost stumble on a rough piece of ground, and Matt and Diane – holding my arms from either side – strengthen their grips so that they can keep me on my feet.

"I'm fine," I tell them.

"You're being very brave," Matt says.

"Do I have a choice?"

"Not really."

As we get closer to the gallows, I realize I can see other figures standing nearby in the darkness. A few dozen people have emerged from the forest, although when I say 'people' I think I really mean ghosts. I still haven't figured this whole mess out just yet, but I'm fairly sure that the dead have gathered to watch as their numbers rise. These might all be people who were executed years ago by Lawrence Radcliffe, and I suppose I understand why they might have some kind of vicarious desire to watch another soul follow in their footsteps. At the same time, I can't help wondering whether they might instead want to stop this insanity.

Reaching the steps that lead up to the platform, I instinctively stop and reach out, touching the damp wood.

"There's no point delaying things," Matt tells me.

I turn to him.

"You'll find peace, I'm sure," he adds. "After all, you seem like someone who's led a good life."

"I wouldn't be so sure about that," I tell him. "There are so many things I still need to do. Things I need to put right, and people I need to help. I owe a lot of apologies and -"

"I'm sorry you didn't get to do that in time," he replies, before stepping closer and trying to push me up the steps. "I'm a father. I have two beautiful children and I have to keep them safe. If you don't go tonight, then that thing in the house will go for my kids instead. Do you understand now why I can't let that happen?"

"If -"

"Move!"

Suddenly he manhandles me up the steps, and before I can fight back I trip and fall, landing directly on the platform. Matt grabs me by the shoulders and drags me across the wood, and then Diane helps him lift me up before they put the noose around my neck and pull it tight.

"Stop!" I shout, finally starting to panic as I realize that I'm running out of time. "You can't do this! Please, you have to let me go!"

"He's watching," Matt replies.

Turning, I look back toward the house and I see that the lights are on in all the rooms. I spot the silhouettes of the two children at one window, and then I see another – taller – silhouette standing at the next window along. Whatever's in that room, it's clearly aware of what's happening, but I can't help thinking that Matt's plan to 'feed' it by killing me is never going to work. That kind of hunger is never truly satisfied, and I really don't think the Hoopers are going to be able to get out of here in time.

"I'm so sorry about this," Matt whispers, leaning closer to my ear.

Before I can reply, I see that the dark ghosts

have gathered all around at the edges of the platform. As they stare up at me, I see their dead eyes burning through the night air, and in that moment I see that many of them are staring at me in expectation. I start to pull against Matt and Diane as they maneuver me into position, but a moment later I look down and see that I'm standing directly on the hatch. I feel a rush of panic fill my body as I look over at the house again. The strange silhouette is still standing at one of the windows, still staring out at us, and I'm starting to realize that Lawrence Radcliffe must still be wanting to experience executions after all these years.

"Wait," I stammer as tears run down my face, "I think I have a better idea. If you just -"

Suddenly the hatch falls beneath me and I drop down. I let out a brief, startled cry before the noose pulls tight around my neck.

CHAPTER TWENTY

THREE HUNDRED YEARS BEFORE that moment, Lawrence Radcliffe stood in the village green and looked out upon the crowd. Having demanded an audience with the locals, he was surprised to find that almost everyone had shown up, although now he found himself wondering just how many of them had been conspiring against him.

"I know what you're doing," he sneered. "Do you think I'm a fool? I know that each and every one of you is in some way complicit with this madness."

He waited, hoping that he'd made his point, yet from the crowd he heard not so much as a murmur. Every face was filled with a strange kind of blankness, and Radcliffe was starting to realize that this village was going to be a far tougher nut to crack than he'd originally believed. At the same time, he also felt that he had an ace up his sleeve, and that he knew exactly how to get through to the hearts and minds of every man, woman and child.

"You have lost one of your number," he reminded them. "Young John Philpott was brutally murdered just outside this village, and as yet his killer has not been apprehended. Do you not spy a connection between this tragedy and the machinations that take place in this wretched place after dark? Can you not comprehend how these things might be linked?"

He hesitated, before holding up the pouch that he himself had removed from the boy's corpse.

"And is this not some part of the scheme?" he asked. "There must be three hundred faces here today. Is there not, among them, one decent soul who will do the right thing and tell me how to stop this madness?"

Again he waited, but he felt no surprise as he saw that everyone was still simply staring at him. Their resilience and unity filled him with righteous fury, but he told himself that soon one of them would crack, that they would have to realize eventually the error of their ways.

"You know where to find me," he said firmly. "And *I* know that there is a good man here, perhaps just one, but one is all I need. Come to me first, and the Lord will forgive all your sins. But come to me second, and you will be seen as just another bad person." He paused again, giving everyone time to reflect upon his words, and in that moment he felt as if he'd truly managed to get his point across. Surely one man would eventually bend to his will. "I look forward to speaking to one of you soon," he added, "and to ridding this village of its detestable curse."

***

Several weeks later, as light rain fell from a graying sky, Radcliffe made his way up the narrow path that led toward the gallows. His legs were aching, but he reminded himself that he was engaged in the Lord's work and that he simply had to keep going. Sooner or later victory would be his.

Spotting a figure up ahead, walking toward him, he quickly recognized Margaret Lantonby, the wife of a local fisherman. Radcliffe slowed his pace, and already his mind was whirring as he recalled that Margaret was renowned in the area as a good church-going woman. He could already tell that she was trying to avoid his gaze, and he felt increasingly confident as he stopped and watched her approach.

"Margaret," he said, hoping that his authority might still carry some weight, "I'm surprised to see you out here today. The weather does not seem to invite stray wandering."

"Good afternoon, Mr. Radcliffe," she murmured, not even looking up at him as she passed. "I bid -"

"Wait a moment," he said suddenly, reaching out and grabbing her arm, forcing her to stop. "We have talked many times in the past, have we not? I believe you have no reason to consider me anything other than a good and honest man."

"Indeed," she replied, although she was still noticeably avoiding his gaze.

"The Philpott boy was buried recently, was he not?" Radcliffe continued. "I used to see him undertaking duties and jobs for his parents, they used to send him out through the village. He was always such a bright and happy young man, and polite as well. Many children are badly behaved, but the little Philpott fellow was absolutely wonderful. I'm sure that all the good people of this place will have thought long and hard about what happened to him."

"I'm sure."

"We still don't know who killed him," he added, and in his mind that statement was now barely a lie. "Or *what* killed him."

"The Lord will -"

"The Lord will reward those who help themselves," Radcliffe told her. "I think you know something, Margaret. I think you know more than you're letting on, and I think you realize you should tell me all of it. Have you any idea how wicked you're being?"

"I am not wicked," she replied, finally glancing at him briefly with tears in her eyes. "Don't say such awful things. I swear I'm a good person."

"Then why do you hide the names of the bad?" he asked, squeezing her arm a little tighter now. "It would be so easy for you to give them up, so why do you not?"

"I have no idea what you're talking about."

"And you speak with a serpent's tongue," he added, "and in so doing you conspire against not only the covenant you made with the Lord, but also against the laws of this fair land. Is that what you want, Margaret? Do you want to keep going along this path toward degeneracy and evil?"

"No!" she blurted out.

"Then tell me what this means!" he snapped, pulling the pouch from his pocket. Turning it around, he showed her the strange symbol depicting horns floating above an eye. "And do not think to lie and say that you know not, because both the Lord and I know that is untrue."

"You're hurting me," she whimpered.

"Not as much as the evil is hurting this town," he replied. "At first I thought it was mere smuggling, but now I realize that something far more sinister is at work here. Tell me, Margaret, are you really willing to work in league with such bad people?"

She opened her mouth to reply, but at the last moment she hesitated. After a few seconds she pulled her arm free and took a step back, and now her expression was filled with fear.

"I'm sorry," she said, as tears began to roll down her cheeks. "You have to believe me, I'm so sorry."

"Don't be sorry," he told her. "Be good. Be right."

"I'm so very sorry."

"That's not enough," he continued, unable to hide a growing sense of frustration. "Margaret, you of all people should realize that it's not enough to -"

"Please be quick," she whimpered, interrupting him. "Don't make him suffer."

"Don't make who suffer?" Radcliffe asked, before hearing a faint sniffing sound coming from somewhere over his shoulder. "Margaret..."

He hesitated, but in that instant he realized that someone was most certainly standing behind him. He began to turn, only to let out a sudden gasp as he felt a blade slice into his back. He looked down just in time to see the blade's tip burst out through the front of his shirt, and already he could feel warm blood starting to run from the wound. He instinctively tried to pull away, but the blade twisted before sliding out and he was powerless to stop himself dropping to his knees.

"I'm sorry!" Margaret sobbed, turning and running away. "Forgive me!"

"Who's there?" Radcliffe gasped, clutching his chest in a desperate last-ditch attempt to stem the flow of blood. "Show yourself!"

Dropping forward, he landed hard on the grass. He tried to get up, but already his body was weakening and after a moment he let out one final, pained gasp. Turning onto his side, he looked up, and in his last seconds he saw the face of his killer. He blinked a couple of times, and then he was gone.

By the time night fell, there was no sign of Lawrence Radcliffe on the spot where he died, save perhaps for some blood that hadn't quite finished soaking into the ground. Six feet further down, however, his body lay buried deep, partially crushed by the huge weight of dirt that pressed against him. His eyes were still open, packed tight with soil, and his mouth was also open in an endless scream. Already, the first worms had found his body and were starting to wriggle their way past his teeth and into the back of his mouth.

CHAPTER TWENTY-ONE

Today...

"NO!"

Suddenly the tension on my neck breaks and I drop down, slamming hard against the grass. Rolling onto my side, I let out a shocked gasp as I look back up through the hatch and hear the sound of two people struggling.

"What are you doing?" Matt hisses. "Are you crazy?"

"Our children are watching!" Diane sobs. "We can't commit murder, especially not in front of them!"

"We're saving them!" he shouts. "Why did you cut her down? Do you want that thing to take Katie and Lance?"

"No, but -"

"Then start thinking like a mother!" he yells, and a moment later I hear the sound of him slapping her hard. "Do you think this is easy for me? I don't want to do it any more than you do, but I know that we don't have a choice! The only thing that matters in this whole world is Katie and Lance!"

Taking advantage of their argument, I crawl out from under the gallows. I know that they'll see me if I try to run back toward the house, so instead I scrambled into the undergrowth at the edge of the forest and throw myself down between two bushes. I reach up and pull hard on the noose that's still attached to my neck, and I start to pull it away, but a moment later I hear footsteps coming toward me.

"Where did she go?" Matt snaps angrily.

"She was right there! Diane whimpers. "Matt, listen, there has to be another way!"

"We need to find her," he replies. "If she goes to the police, we're completely screwed. They'll never believe her story, but they'll still start poking around and we can't afford that. She can't have got far, though, so we can still find her. You go that way, and I'll check over here."

"I'm not going to let you hurt her!"

"I won't let you be involved this time," he says firmly. "That was a mistake, and I'm sorry. Just help me find her this one last time, and after that I'll do everything else by myself." He pauses as I stay completely still and quiet down here in the bushes. "You know I love you, Diane," he adds. "You know I'm only doing all of this because I'm determined to keep our family safe. Please, Diane, everything I've done since this whole mess started has been about looking after all of us. I need you to remember that."

"I do," she replies, although she sounds a little uncertain. "I just couldn't kill her in cold blood."

"You won't have to," he tells her, "because I'll handle that next time. Just help me track her down."

As they hurry off through the forest, I sit up and try to work out which way to go next. I quickly pull the noose away from my neck and throw it aside, and then I get to my feet. My first thought is that I should simply go back down past the house, but as I look that way I realize that I'll be completely out in the open. I can't ignore the possibility that Matt or Diane might double back around, so instead I start picking my way through the undergrowth, staying as close as possible to the edge of the forest so that I don't completely lose my way. As far as I know, this stretch of densely-wooded forest could stretch all the way to Grove Weld, so I really don't want to end up losing my bearings.

Stopping after a moment, I realize that I should perhaps head back down to Davis Drive after all. When I turn and look back, however, I see that while the gallows might have disappeared, Lance and Katie have emerged through the back gate and are standing on the slope. I really don't know that I can trust them, so I turn and start pushing through the bushes, daring to go a little deeper into the forest while making sure that I don't lose track of which way I'm going. I tell myself that if I just head straight on, sooner or later I should come out toward the rear of the area around the church.

***

Half an hour later, I continue to make my way through pitch darkness, although I'm starting to worry that I might be lost after all. I trip for what feels like the hundredth time, and then I stop for a moment and take a look around.

I should be out of the forest by now.

How have I managed to go the wrong way?

"Mercy!" Matt's voice calls out in the distance. "We just want to talk to you!"

I hear Diane's voice, and see seems even further away. A moment later I hear Matt again, and I'm relieved to note that he too seems to be heading in the wrong direction.

"Come on," I mutter under my breath as I

duck down under some low-hanging branches and try to work out exactly which way I should go next. "You can do this. You might not have a huge amount of experience out in the sticks, but that doesn't mean you can't look after yourself."

Although I believe those words, I have to admit that I'd love Jessica to show up right now. She has a tendency to just get things done, and I figure her no-nonsense attitude would probably get us out of the forest in double-quick time. Then again, I know that I really can't keep relying on her to always come charging to the rescue, and I also know that lately she seems far too busy to even notice what I'm doing; I keep telling myself that there's no need to worry, but deep down I know it's not like her to stay so quiet for so long.

I push past some more branches, and then I stop in my tracks as I hear a faint rustling sound coming from nearby.

Looking around, I tell myself that there's no way that either Matt or Diane could possibly have made it back this way so quickly. A fraction of a second later I hear a cracking sound, as if somebody stepped on a twig, and then I look the other way and spot a figure standing just a few feet away, glaring at me from the darkness.

"Who are you?" I gasp, pulling back until I bump into one of the other trees.

"Are you a good person?" he asks.

"What do you want?" I snap.

"Are you a good person?" he asks again, and this time he steps forward, allowing me to see his pale features and his cold dead eyes. "If you are, you must surely help me to uncover the truth about this wretched place."

"Are -"

I hesitate for a moment. I know full well that this guy is dead, and I already suspect that I might know his name.

"Are you... Lawrence Radcliffe?" I ask cautiously.

"I am charged with tidying up the mess that has been made of this place," he replies, his voice sounding harsh and damaged as he continues to stare at me. "I was sent to deal with the smugglers and all the other ne'er-do-wells and as the Lord is my witness, I shall not rest until my duty has been fully discharged."

"Right," I stammer, as I try to understand what he's doing out here in the forest. "So you don't just hang out in the wardrobe, huh?"

"I don't understand your words," he replies. "I walk the forest, for I know that somewhere out here I can find proof of my suspicions."

"You walk the forest?" I say, as I try to put all the pieces together. "So what you're saying is that... it's not you in that house, is it?"

"My bones are buried nearby," he explains,

"but I cannot rest with them, not when this wretched village remains under malign influence. Can you not feel the evil in the air all around you? There's something in this forest, something that should have been dealt with a long time ago but the people of this cursed place refused to cooperate with me! In life, I was never able to get to the truth, but in death... I believe I have uncovered at least part of what truly happened. Tell me, young lady, do you believe in ghosts?"

"I'd be hard-pressed not to," I reply, "given that I'm talking to one right now."

"I am but the ghost of a man," he points out, before raising his right hand and pointing past me, "but do you believe that there can be ghosts of other things? Of things, perhaps, that do not have a soul as you and I would understand it?"

I open my mouth to reply to him, but at the last second I realize that he's looking past me. I turn to look over my shoulder, and to my shock I realize that whereas a moment ago there was nothing to see except more trees, now – bathed in a batch of moonlight – I see what appears to be an old stone-walled chapel.

CHAPTER TWENTY-TWO

"WHAT *IS* THIS PLACE?" I whisper as I step past a few more trees and approach the edge of the clearing. "How did it get here? I swear it wasn't here a moment ago."

"Indeed," Radcliffe replies, following a few steps behind me, "but you see it now, do you not?"

Making my way toward the front of the building, where a wooden door firm and tall, I reach out and feel the stones at its side. I know this building can't really be here right now, but it certainly feels very real and the wall remains very firm and resolute even as I begin to push gently. I tell myself that there's no way an entire building can come back as a kind of ghost, but I have to admit that the gallows felt very real; in fact, I can still feel a faint soreness around my neck, no doubt caused by the rope.

"I confess that during my lifetime," Radcliffe continues, "I allowed anger and fury to corrupt my vision. I became almost a madman, railing against unseen enemies rather than taking the time to confront them properly. Eventually I did a very bad thing, I killed a young boy, and for that I can never be forgiven. Yet in death I have found a level of clarity that I was missing before, and I believe that I can yet help to drive the evil out of Candleward."

I push against the wall for a moment longer, before turning to him.

"For that, however," he adds mournfully, "I need help."

"You're not the entity in that house," I reply.

"I am not. But there is a presence in Candleward, something that has been here for a very long time. Indeed, it has lasted for much longer than any ordinary man should."

"So it's another ghost?"

"I fear that it is something darker than that," he explains. "Something with plans that threaten the very foundation of this village. Something truly dreadful and powerful."

"Dreadful and powerful," I reply cautiously, "but also trapped in a wardrobe?"

"I do not claim to understand everything," he tells me, "but I know that this entity has gathered worshipers over the years, and I am quite sure that these worshipers built this very chapel for the purpose of practicing their dark arts. The chapel was destroyed before my time, and I did not see it in its present state. Indeed, I am surprised that *you* see it now, but I can only assume that you have some unusual ability to detect the presence of the dead."

"Something like that," I tell him as I turn to the chapel again. I look at the door, and then I reach out for the handle, which to my surprise turns fairly easily. "You said that this is a chapel. I've never heard anything about an old chapel having stood out here before."

"I doubt that many are aware of its existence," he continues. "There are certainly very few people who ever make the journey to this spot. And those who *do* come here tend to ignore the ruins, as if they see nothing of interest."

I hesitate, before pushing the door open. All I see on the inside is darkness, but I can already feel the cold air against my face.

"What's in here?" I ask cautiously.

"I do not know."

I turn to him.

"I cannot enter," he continues. "I have tried many times, but it is simply impossible. I don't know if my faith keeps me out, or the sins I have committed, but I am physically incapable of stepping inside this apparition. And while I have waited out here for so very long, you are the first person who has seen me and interacted with me. If you can enter this place and prove that I am correct, then I might finally be able to save all of Candleward."

"You make it sound so simple," I reply, pushing the door open a little further.

I can see inside a little better now. The windows are old and dirty, letting in only a fraction of the moonlight, but I can at least make out the backs of row after row of pews. This definitely has the feel of an old church, and although I can't quite see the far end I'm fairly sure that there's probably some kind of altar. At the same time, I still can't quite believe that an actual chapel could have once stood out here, only to end up being destroyed and lost to history. There are several local history groups in the area and I'm sure that I would have heard about this place by now.

"Something bad happened here once," Radcliffe tells me. "Long ago. Something terrible. Can you not feel the pain and fear in the air?"

"Just give me a couple of minutes," I reply, as I step forward and find that – unlike my new friend – I seem to be perfectly capable of entering the chapel. "You're right about one thing. Something in the air here feels very wrong."

***

As I take a few more steps toward the back row of pews, I look around and see tall stained-glass windows towering above me on either side. Whoever built this place, they certainly went to a lot of trouble and there's a very powerful atmosphere here. I don't see anyone inside, and I don't feel any kind of presence either, but at the same time I'm sure I'm sensing some kind of tremor in the air.

"This whole building is a ghost," I whisper, barely able to believe the words that are coming out of my mouth. I turn and look back out at Radcliffe. "You were right, but I don't understand how."

He steps forward, only to immediately stop and pull back.

"You still can't come inside, huh?" I continue.

"I don't know whether that's a curse or a blessing," he replies.

"Me neither."

Turning, I start making my way along the aisle that runs between the pews. I glance at the seats on either side, and although I don't see any ghostly figures sitting nearby I can't help but imagine the days when this place would have had a congregation. My footsteps are echoing in the cold air as I head toward the altar at the chapel's far end, and now I can see a raised platform with some kind of lectern in the middle. This definitely doesn't feel like any kind of Christian church, and there are certainly no crosses or crucifixes around, but as I reach the edge of the platform I spot a large symbol carved into the stone wall.

A pair of horns above an eye.

"I think you might have been onto something," I call out, before glancing back at Radcliffe. He's still watching me from outside. "I think this place is linked to that little boy, and to all the stuff you thought was going on hundreds of years ago."

"I always prayed that I might be wrong," he tells me.

Heading up the steps, I reach the middle of the altar and examine the lectern more closely. There's certainly a spot where a book could once have been placed, although there's no sign of any book now. I feel as if I'm being watched from all sides, but after glancing around for a moment I realize that this sensation might have been caused by the church itself, as if the building has a kind of presence that's dominating every breath that I take. I know I might be getting ahead of myself a little, and that I shouldn't take Radcliffe's claims to heart just yet, but I still can't shake the feeling that this ghostly chapel is unlike any other place I've been to since I came to Candleward.

"What do you see?" Radcliffe calls out to me from the steps at the front. "Please, you must tell me everything!"

"How old did you say this place was again?" I ask, as I peer more closely at some scratch-marks on the lectern.

"Centuries," he tells me. "Perhaps for almost as long as Candleward itself has existed. Perhaps even longer."

"That would mean that something has been bubbling away beneath the surface for all this time," I whisper, touching the scratch-marks and feeling their depth against my fingertips. "This entire place might have been affected by whoever built the chapel in the first place."

"Can't you go into more detail?" Radcliffe asks, and he sounds extremely impatient now. "I've waited so long to know what happened in this chapel."

"I don't know," I say as I look toward the door again, "but -"

In that instant, I suddenly see scores of shadowy figures sitting on the pews, staring straight at me. I tell myself that I have to be wrong, but before I can call out to Radcliffe again the chapel's door swings shut, slamming loudly and sealing me inside.

CHAPTER TWENTY-THREE

"HEY!" I CALL OUT, hoping against hope that he can still hear me. "Radcliffe, are you there?"

I wait, but I don't hear an answer. Instead, I look once again at the figures sitting on the pews. They seem almost to be expecting something, as if they think I'm about to launch into a sermon. I don't dare to step down from the altar yet and walk along the aisle, in case by moving I disturb these people. So far they seem content to simply stare at me, although I know I can't simply stand up here forever.

"Hey," I say again, more softly this time. "Does anyone here want to fill me in on exactly what's happening?"

Again I wait, but so far the shadowy figures seem so vague and ill-defined, and I'm almost tempted to believe that they're barely really here at all. I step away from the lectern and back over to the steps that lead down to the aisle; I really don't like the idea of getting too close to these people, yet at the same time I know that I need to figure out what they're doing here. I force myself to head down the steps, and then I step over to the end of the front pew and look down at the figure before me.

This is a man, I can tell that much, although his features are difficult to pick out. He's staring straight up at me, and a moment later when I look all around I realize that every figure is staring at me; that doesn't exactly make me feel too much better, but when I look down at the man again I tell myself that I should at least be able to get him to talk to me.

"My name's Mercy," I explain, hoping for some kind of breakthrough. "Mercy Willow. I'm not really sure what's going on here, but can you tell me what this place is?"

He doesn't answer, so after a moment I crouch down in front of him. Sure enough, his eyes follow me, so at least I can be sure now that he's aware of my presence. In my experience, however, ghosts tend to have an agenda, and I can't quite work out why all these people are content to simply sit here like this. They're all definitely waiting for something, and after a moment I realize that based on everything Radcliffe told me – plus the style of clothing I can just make out on these people – they might very well have been waiting for many hundreds of years. I've encountered ghosts in the past, of course, but I still don't quite understand what could motivate so *many* ghosts to hang around in one place for so long.

"I want to help you," I tell the man, trotting out a line I've used plenty of times in the past. "But for that to happen, I need to know what you're doing here. I need to know what you want, and how I can fix things for you."

Watching his face, I see no trace of a reaction. He must be able to hear me, yet evidently he has no desire to speak. In that case, I'm going to have to try a slightly different approach.

"If -"

"You won't get anywhere with them."

Startled, I turn and see a figure standing at the top of the steps. The figure moves a little closer and I'm shocked to see Diane Hooper staring back down at me.

"We've tried," she continues. "I mean, *I've* tried. I really don't think Matt's too interested in the details."

"What are you doing here?" I ask, getting to my feet and looking around.

"Relax, Matt's not with me," she says as I turn to her again. "He's gone back to the house to check on the children. I told him I'd keep looking for you, although to be honest I had a pretty good idea that I'd find you right here. Did the ghost of that Radcliffe guy lead you to the door?"

"Have you seen him too?"

"I have, many times," she says as she makes her way down the steps, "and every time he seems to think it's the first. He always tells me that no-one else has been able to see him, and that no-one else has been able to see this chapel. I can't be sure, but I suspect that his mind isn't quite all there. Then again, he's several hundred years old, so I guess we shouldn't be too harsh on him."

She holds up a small wooden crucifix that she's clutching in her hands.

"Is it foolish that I brought this?" she adds. "It seems so simple, I can't believe that it could ever afford any of us any real protection. I don't even believe in these things, but my parents did so I suppose I might as well carry it around in case it helps."

"What do you know about this place?" I ask.

"I know it was built hundreds of years ago by some people who had a few rather odd beliefs," she explains. "They were followers of a man who came here and filled their heads with all sorts of crazy ideas. Have you ever heard of Warrington Chase?"

"I -"

Before I can finish, I realize that the name

rings some bells. Farrar has been working for an institute that was founded by Chase.

"He was a man who wanted to live forever," Diane continues. "He thought he'd cracked the secret, too. He might have done, but he failed to specify *where* he wanted to do this living. By all accounts, he was screaming very loudly as his body was dragged off to some other world. That would have been the end of it, except he left behind some books and notes. A few other people began to wonder whether they could modify Chase's work and have another try, but first they needed to know exactly what Chase had done wrong. For them, the simplest approach was to ask him."

"How?"

"By summoning his spirit back to this world. Which apparently is perfectly possible, but they forgot that Chase would be absolutely desperate to stick around by any means possible. This chapel was used for the services, and little by little the congregation managed to start cracking open the same door that Warrington Chase had disappeared into. I'm sure there were more than a few dissenting voices, warning about the consequences of what they were attempting, but they would have been drowned out by those who wanted to keep pushing on. And they *did* push on, until finally one day in this very church they went too far."

"What happened?" I ask, before looking around once more at the shadowy figures. "Did they all die here?"

"That's where the story becomes a little muddled," she replies. "According to some accounts, the members of the congregation all spontaneously committed suicide after they realized what was happening. According to others, something came into this world – albeit briefly – and killed them all. I've never quite been able to get to the bottom of it all, but my best guess is that the truth is somewhere in the middle. Whatever happened, the chapel burned down and some of the locals chose to demolish what little was left. After that, everyone in Candleward was happy to forget that the place had ever existed in the first place."

"You make it sound like some kind of cult," I tell her.

"It might well have been."

"And then it was all covered up?"

"That seems to have been the prevailing attitude," she continues, "but I'm not sure that something like this can ever be truly brushed under the carpet. The chapel itself seems to insist on still existing, although I doubt that's quite the way it works."

"How do you know all this?" I ask. "I've done a lot of research and I never uncovered anything about this chapel. It's not on any of the old maps, and I'm sure it's not mentioned in the historical records."

"I know about it because I've spoken to someone who was there."

"Who was *where*?"

"Here," she continues with a faint smile, as if this answer is the most obvious in the world. "You're really struggling to figure all of this out, aren't you? To be fair, Matt's the same. He's got all these theories, and I let him get on with things, but that's really because I need to keep him distracted. Matt's a good man and he cares so much about our family, but at the end of the day sometimes those qualities can lead a guy down the wrong rabbit hole."

"What do you mean?" I ask, as I start to realize that there's really something very unsettling about her smile. "What exactly are you trying to achieve here?"

"Warrington Chase is coming back to this world," she tells me, "and all that he requires now is a body. A vessel. He's tried a few times over the years, but people have always fought back against him. This time, however, he's going to be welcomed willingly and with open arms. He's going to take my son Lance's body, and then we'll all share in the glory of his return. If you think about it, this is really a win-win situation for everyone."

CHAPTER TWENTY-FOUR

"STAY STRONG," FATHER ELLIS said firmly as he stood at the lectern, three hundred years before the days of Mercy Willow and Diane Hooper. "I urge all of you to stay strong and wait for the moment!"

He heard a few murmured words of concern rising from the congregation, but for the most part Ellis felt sure that he had the situation under control. The entire chapel was shuddering slightly, hinting at the tremendous power that would soon be unleashed, but Ellis knew without a shadow of a doubt that he was on the verge of attaining true greatness. Having teased the edges of the unknown for so long, he felt sure that he'd finally made contact with the great prophet Warrington Chase and that soon the world would be changed forever.

Suddenly he heard a rustling sound, and he looked up just in time to see a woman racing out of the chapel.

"Stop!" he shouted, although he was too late. The woman was now long gone. "The rest of you must not follow that fool," he continued. "Those who cower in fear will be punished. Those who remain firm and resolute will be rewarded for all eternity. There is no greater certainty than the fact that we are on the proper path to righteousness!"

He looked from face to face, and for the most part he saw stoic determination staring back at him.

"We are on the verge of greatness," he explained, before holding up the battered knife he'd been keeping on the lectern. "When I used this very blade to rid us of that troublesome Radcliffe man, I did it because I knew that we couldn't let anything stand in our way. Warrington Chase has spent time in the afterlife, and when he returns he will have so much to tell us. We lucky few will learn all the truths and secrets of the world, and with those secrets we shall go forth and be amongst the mighty! And then -"

Before he could get another word out, a man rose from his seat near the front of the congregation and fled, racing along the aisle and quickly disappearing outside.

"Remain strong," Ellis snarled. "I'm warning you, anyone who falters at this late stage will be punished in the eternal fires of -"

A second woman clambered from her seat and ran, and this time two other women from the back row joined her.

"I will not have this!" Ellis roared.

Before the three women could get outside, the church's door slammed shut. They immediately tried the handle, only to find that the door was now sealed.

"The time is upon us," Ellis whispered softly, as a smile grew across his face. "Our benefactor is about to return to this world, and when he does, he will be given a list of the names of the faithful."

The three women turned to him.

"And the unfaithful," he added, his voice filled with a growing sense of menace.

"Please let us go!" one of the women sobbed. "We just want to go home!"

"You *are* home," Ellis replied. "Any moment now, Warrington Chase will return and a new dawn will begin. That is when the non-believers will realize the errors of their ways and -"

Suddenly one of the women screamed, and at that moment Ellis felt a burning sensation on his left leg. Looking down, he saw to his horror that his leg was on fire, and the flames had already begun to spread up and across his body. He held out his hands as if he couldn't believe what he was seeing, and then – as he looked out once again at the congregation – he opened his mouth and smoke bellowed from the back of his throat.

"Stay strong!" he gasped, barely able to get any words out at all. "Listen to me, you must be -"

In an instant he let out a pained cry, and he clutched the sides of the lectern as more and more flames engulfed his body. A moment later he slumped forward, barely even visible anymore at the heart of the inferno, and already the remaining members of the congregation were rushing to the door and trying desperately to get it open. Ellis began to scream, his anguished voice filling the chapel as he leaned further forward and the lectern toppled over, sending the burning man crashing down the steps until he landed in a fiery heap on the floor below.

"Run!" Margaret Lantonby shouted as she and two other women tried desperately to push the door open. "We must -"

In that instant her right arm burst into flames, as did the bodies of several of the people around her. As screams began to ring out, everyone began to throw themselves at the door with such force that many were trampled. A sense of panic began to spread, and now every man and woman in the chapel was burning as they tried frantically to find some way out of the building. Soon the air was filled with the sound of crackling flesh, and as each body crumpled to the floor another soul climbed over them and tried to smash the door down. With each passing second, however, the number of moving bodies began to dwindle, until only a few remained pressed against the door in one last attempt to break free.

Finally, as flames ate the flesh from her face, Margaret Lantonby looked up toward the chapel's high ceiling and screamed.

***

"What happened here?" Jonathan Donachie asked the following morning, as he and several other men from the village made their way between the trees, approaching the smoking remains of the chapel. "How can this be?"

"I warned you all," Thomas Parker said, following a little way back. "I told you something bad was happening out here, that we shouldn't have let these people live in our community, but no-one listened to me."

"We all saw the flames last night," Donachie replied, stopping and watching as lingering trails of smoke rose from the rubble. "Base superstition kept us in our homes until the light of morning. If we'd come out here sooner -"

"We couldn't have saved them," Marcus Overford said, interrupting him. "Whatever happened out here is a tragedy to be sure, but don't ignore the fact that we're now rid of a dangerous element that was festering in our community. I hate to say this, but I happen to think that for all his faults, Lawrence Radcliffe might have been correct. We all kept our heads turned for far too long."

"How many people are unaccounted for today?" Donachie asked.

"Fifty-three, I believe," one of the other men suggested.

"Fifty-three lost souls," Donachie continued, his voice filled with sadness as he watched the chapel's ruins. "We all knew that they were up to no good. We all heard the rumors about this cult."

"Was it really a cult?" Parker asked.

"I'd say so," Donachie replied. "They were trying to resurrect a dead man. I don't know about the rest of you, but I intend to go to church this morning and pray harder than I've ever prayed before. We allowed this sacrilege to exist in the heart of our community, and I am not sure that the Lord will ever forgive us. All we can do is try our best to atone for these sins."

"At least they failed," Parker said.

The others turned to him.

"*Clearly* they failed," he continued, pointing

toward what was left of the chapel. "There's nothing here except the ruins of this strange little place, and that at least saves us the trouble of having to tear it down from scratch. If you ask me, we should be thankful that we seem to have emerged unscathed."

"You might very well be correct," Donachie told him. "The time for talking is over. We must not let this heathen place become a stain on our village. I suggest that we knock down the rest of this chapel and salt the ground, and then we must pretend that it was never here. As for the dead, we shall bury their bones somewhere and grieve for them while recognizing that they allowed their souls to become tempted. It is my utmost hope that – a century from now – no-one will know that such an awful thing ever happened here."

"I for one would like to forget all of it," Parker said darkly, and the rest of the men immediately muttered their agreement. "We're good people in these parts. Our names shouldn't be dragged down just because one man managed to rile up a few idiots."

"Let's not call people idiots," Donachie reminded him. "We should get to work, though. The sooner this whole sorry mess is forgotten, the better for everyone concerned."

CHAPTER TWENTY-FIVE

"WARRINGTON CHASE IS DEAD," I tell Diane, as I look into her eyes and start to see a glint of madness. "Whatever happened here all those years ago -"

"What happened here was a tragedy," she replies, "but one that can be undone. The very presence of this chapel tonight is proof of that. The building knows that it still has a role to play. I don't know what mistake those fools made when they first tried to bring Chase back, but there won't be any mistakes this time. This time we're going to succeed."

"I don't think that's a very good idea," I say as I try to work out how I'm going to get away from this lunatic. I definitely need to get Farrar involved in this mess. "Why don't we sleep on it and have another chat tomorrow? How does midday sound? At your place?"

"I won't let you get in the way," she says, taking another step toward me. "You have to understand that this is going to be the culmination of such a lot of work. If you insist on getting in our way, then I'm afraid I'll have to silence you. Permanently."

"But -"

Stopping suddenly, I realize that one aspect of her story makes no sense at all.

"If you want to silence me," I say cautiously, "then why did you stop Matt hanging me? If you hadn't stepped in, I'd be dead by now and you'd be free to do whatever you want."

I wait for an answer, but I can already tell from the look in her eyes that something's wrong. In fact, the more I watch Diane, the more I realize that she doesn't really seem like Diane Hooper at all; there's a strange calmness about her demeanor, coupled with a kind of icy stare that makes me feel as if I'm being analyzed. If anything, I'm feeling more and more certain that this can't possibly be the same woman who saved me on the gallows.

"I'm going to try to find a way out of here," I say cautiously. "How did you get in, by the way?

Is there some kind of back door?"

"You keep sticking your nose in, don't you?" she replies, stepping toward me.

I immediately start backing away, before making my way along one of the rows.

"You don't understand anything," she continues. "I almost admire you, in a way. Most people would notice their own ignorance and perhaps temper their actions, but you just throw yourself into everything you see. I've encountered people like you before, and it never ends well for them. Even at Torfork Tower, you couldn't resist getting involved."

"Torfork Tower?" Reaching the end of the row, I look past the altar. I'm sure there must be another way out back there, although I know I really need to get this right the first time. "Why are you talking about Torfork Tower?"

"When you dealt with the ghosts there," she replies. "There was that idiotic man who thought he could follow in my footsteps. And that stupid girl who actually believed that she could control the ceremony. I honestly don't know where you find these idiots."

"How do you know about all of that?" I ask.

"Because I was there," she says with a grin.

"You and Matt didn't even move to

Candleward until after everything at Torfork Tower happened," I point out.

"Now you're being intentionally idiotic, aren't you?" she replies, edging closer to me even as I continue to back away. "You know who you're talking to right now, don't you? You must know that when those idiots burned this chapel to the ground all those years ago, they actually succeeded in bringing me back to life. They just didn't do it in quite the way that they intended, and I've been rather... bouncing around ever since."

"Warrington Chase," I whisper as I begin to realize exactly who's possessing Diane's body right now. "You survived all this time."

"I tried being dead, and I didn't like it," Diane continues, even though I'm certain now that it's Chase's mind speaking through her voice. "I just need a more permanent body. When those houses were built on Davis Drive, they were just close enough for me to reach out from these ruins and interfere with the minds of the inhabitants. Most of them managed to push me away, some of them didn't even realize what was happening, but finally I've lucked upon some fools who are easily controlled. I just need to pick one of them for the long haul."

"Why did you hide in their wardrobe?"

"I didn't," she snarls. "That poor pathetic magistrate barely remembers a thing he does."

"You mean Lawrence Radcliffe?"

"His bones are buried under that house, so he's drawn back there most of the time. His mind is completely shot, he really doesn't seem to be able to carry a thought from one moment to the next. At first I was a little worried about him, I feared he might interfere, but eventually I realized that he was nothing more than an idiot. In fact, I find his attempts to help people rather amusing."

I look toward the area behind the altar.

"Are you thinking of making a run for it?" Diane asks. "I was in Matt Hooper's body on the gallows, and this pathetic woman got in the way. I won't let that happen again." She holds the crucifix up ahead, clutching it in her right hand. "I've waited so long to take a body again, but I'm starting to think that there's no need to pick and choose. I might as well take all four of the Hoopers and just use them as I see fit."

"You're forgetting something," I tell her, as I still try to judge my escape to perfection.

"And what's that?"

"I'm going to stop you."

In that moment, I turn and try to run toward the rear of the chapel, only for Diane to rush after me. She grabs my arm and pulls me back before throwing me against the steps. I slam down hard and roll to the floor, and a fraction of a second later Diane hauls me up by the scruff of my neck and turns me around as she leans down and stares into my eyes. She's still holding the crucifix, clutching it tight as if she's about to use it to bludgeon me to death.

"You're not going to stop anything," she sneers. "I've been watching you for a while and I know you have a habit of interfering, but this time you've gone too far. I've waited a long time for my chance to truly return to the world, and I'm not going to let you stand in my way."

"But if -"

"You stopped me once," she continues, leaning even closer as I reach out and try to find something – anything – I might be able to use as a weapon. "Do you think I didn't notice you down in the cliff chamber? The Danvers girl was an idiot but I would have been able to use her, and instead you ripped the heart from her chest. Do you really think that I'm willing to accept any more delays? I have yearned for so long to feel my soul fill a body of flesh and blood. The Hooper family are perfect. They're weak and easily controlled, and they each have certain qualities and advantages that I can use to my benefit."

Reaching past her, I feel something hard and solid near the altar.

"You're forgetting something else," I stammer.

"And what's that?"

"The lectern."

"What -"

Before she can get another word out, I bring the lectern crashing down against the back of her head. She lets out a faint cry as she tumbles down onto the stone floor, but as I scramble to safety I turn and see that she's been knocked out cold. Taking a deep breath, I stumble to my feet as I try to work out exactly what's happening here. If that really *was* the ghost of Warrington Chase possessing her body, then at least he won't be able to do anything with her for a while, although I quickly remember that he claimed to be able to possess the rest of the family as well. If that's the case, then they're still in danger back at the house and I might not have much time left if I'm going to save them.

I turn to run to the door, before spotting something resting on the floor. Reaching down, I pick up Diane's wooden crucifix.

"I might need this," I murmur as I turn and

hurry along the aisle. "You never know."

CHAPTER TWENTY-SIX

BY THE TIME I get back to the edge of the forest and spot the houses on Davis Drive again, I feel as if I might be about to collapse. I pause for a moment to lean against a tree and try to get some strength back, but I'm out of breath and I still don't really understand what's happening.

Ahead, the platform of the gallows has disappeared once more, leaving only a few stumps of wood poking out from the ground.

I set off again, heading for the gate that leads into the garden of the Hoopers' house. I know I have to be careful, and I slow my pace as I reach the gate and see that it's been left partially open. Peering through the gap, I see that many of the lights are on inside the house, but so far there's no sign of anyone. I creep past the gate and start making my way along the path that leads toward the back door, while watching the windows in case Matt or one of the children might suddenly appear.

After all, I have no idea which of them might be possessed by Warrington Chase right now, and I can't just assume that it'll be Matt.

Reaching the door, I find that this too has been left partially open. I can't shake the feeling that I'm almost being invited inside, but at the same time I'm worried that Chase might be about to do something truly awful to them all. As I step into the kitchen and look around, I can't deny that the place looks fairly normal, and there's certainly nothing to indicate that a malevolent centuries-old spirit is lurking in the shadows. There's also no sign of Matt and the children, however, and as I reach the hallway and look toward the foot of the stairs I start to wonder whether anyone's home at all.

"Hello?" I call out finally, figuring that I need to speak up. "Is anyone here?"

No-one replies, so I make my way to the stairs and look up. I'm worried that Matt might attack me at any moment, and I can't help but note that my only form of defense right now is a wooden crucifix, but I figure that it's better than nothing. I hesitate, watching the landing for a moment longer, and then I start to slowly make my way up toward the top floor.

"Warrington Chase," I continue, "can you

hear me right now? Because if you can, you have to know that this isn't going to work. No-one's going to let you just take control of an entire family like this. If we talk, there might be some other way I can help you, but if we don't talk..."

Stopping as I reach the landing, I realize that I can hear a faint sobbing sound nearby. I step over to the doorway that leads into Lance's room, and I'm shocked to see Katie kneeling on the floor and staring into the open wardrobe. I wait to see what she's doing, but after a few seconds I see tears running down her face as a frail voice whispers something from the wardrobe's interior.

"You have to be strong," the voice says, "and you have to be careful. You need to run. Get your entire family out of here before that wretched thing strikes again."

As I step into the room, my right foot presses against a loose floorboard. Katie turns to me, clearly terrified, and then she gets to her feet.

"I'm trying!" she whimpers. "You don't understand, I'm trying really hard!"

"What are you trying to do?" I ask.

"I don't know how to stop him!" she yells, racing out of the room before I have a chance to stop her.

As I hear her hurrying into one of the other rooms, I look at the wardrobe and see that the ghost of Lawrence Radcliffe is sitting on the floor and staring up at me. He's curled into a ball as if he's terrified, and after taking a couple more steps forward I realize I can feel his fear hanging all around me in the air.

"I've tried to warn them," he sobs. "All of them, all the families who've come here, and in the past I've managed to keep them strong. This time, though, something's different." He pauses for a moment. "You went into the chapel. Tell me, what did you see?"

"I saw ghosts," I tell him. "Lots of ghosts."

"But did you see *him*!" he hisses. "Did you see the one who started it all! Did you see Warrington Chase!"

"I heard him," I reply, although I still can't quite believe that these words are leaving my lips. "I think. He's possessing people as part of some attempt to -"

"I was right all along!" he continues, cutting me off. "I was too foolish to identify the precise nature of the threat, but I knew this village was infected with an evil that it could never shrug off! Now that evil has taken root and I fear it can never be removed. The only solution is to destroy all of Candleward and salt the ground, and pray that this is enough."

"That sounds... extreme," I point out, before hearing a series of heavy thuds coming from one of the other bedrooms. I turn and look out toward the landing. "There's another way to fix this, and I'm going to figure it out."

***

Once I'm back out on the landing, I realize that the thudding sound is actually some kind of scuffle. I step over to the door that leads into the master bedroom, and I see that Lance is frantically holding onto his sister and trying to restrain her as she frantically pulls away.

"What are you guys doing?" I ask.

"We have to stay here!" Lance snaps angrily, clearly struggling to keep hold of Katie. "Dad told us to stay in this room and wait for him!"

"Where's your father now?"

"He went out," Lance continues, sounding a little breathless now. "He said -"

Suddenly Katie bites him hard on the arm, causing him to let out a cry of pain and pull back. Taking her chance, Katie scrambles free and races across the room, slamming into me before turning and pointing at her brother.

"It's him!" she shouts. "That's the man! He's not my brother!"

"I *am* your brother!" Lance yells angrily. "Why do you keep saying that? I just want to help you and keep you safe until Dad comes back!"

"That's not Lance," Katie whispers, tugging

at my sleeve. "He keeps saying that he is, but I know he isn't. The man in the wardrobe warned me that someone was going to try to hurt my family, and he told me that I can't trust anyone."

"Why are you being so stupid?" Lance asks as he gets to his feet and steps toward us. "Katie, it's obviously me, so why do you keep saying that I'm someone else?"

"Because the man warned us!" she shouts.

"Okay, calm down," I reply, hoping to talk some sense into them both. "We're going to figure this all out but -"

"Mummy!"

Suddenly Katie rushes away from me, and I turn just in time to see her put her arms around Diane. I immediately pull back, but in that moment I see that the expression on Diane's face is very different to before; she has a nasty cut on her forehead, no doubt caused by the lectern that fell on her, but she looks extremely confused and I can already tell that she's no longer possessed by the spirit of Warrington Chase. If that's the case, however, that means that Chase must be somewhere else.

"I don't know what's happening," Diane tells me, as tears fill her eyes, "but Matt told me to come up here and I think something's wrong with him."

"We all need to get out of the house," I reply as she steps further into the room, "and -"

Before I can get another word out, I spot Matt standing out on the landing. I briefly make eye contact with him, but in that moment he slams the door shut and I hear a key turning in the lock. Stepping past Diane, I try the door, only to find that it's locked, and a moment later I hear the sound of Matt hurrying back down the stairs.

"He's locked us in," I say, before turning to Diane and the two children. "Why would he do that?"

"I don't know," Diane replies, "but he's acting very strangely." She pauses. "He's not the only one. I have this bump on my head, and I woke up out in the forest but I don't remember what happened. It's as if I've been blacking out."

"That's when you've been possessed by Warrington Chase."

"Who?"

"There's no time to explain now," I tell her, "but -"

"Mummy, look!" Katie shouts, pointing toward the bottom of the door. "Mummy, there's a fire!"

Turning, I see to my horror that she's right. Thick black smoke is reaching under the door and starting to fill the room, and a fraction of a second later I realize that I can also make out a crackling fiery glow flickering out on the landing. Spotting more smoke nearby, I turn and see that some is breaking through the floorboards and starting to fill the room's other end, and I realize in an instant that this can only mean one thing.

"He's burning the house down," Diane stammers, as she pulls the children close. "He's burning it down with us inside. He's trying to kill us all!"

CHAPTER TWENTY-SEVEN

"MATT!" DIANE SHOUTS, POUNDING on the door yet again as more and more smoke fills the room. "Why are you doing this? Let us out of here!"

"It must be because of Warrington Chase," I stammer, holding the front of my shirt up in a desperate attempt to protect my mouth and nose from the worst of the smoke, "but I don't get it. Chase wants bodies to possess, why would he go to so much trouble and then destroy those bodies?"

"I'm sorry!" Matt shouts suddenly from the other side of the door. "You have to understand that this is the only way!"

"Open the door!" Diane yells, pulling frantically on the handle.

"I can't!" he whimpers. "You saw what I nearly did tonight, Diane. This thing has our entire family in its grip, and it won't let go. I can't let it fill our souls and poison us and make us do awful things, so there's only one other choice. While I've got a clear head, I have to save us all, and there's only one way to do that. I'm so sorry."

"This isn't the answer!" I call out, hurrying to the door and trying the handle myself. "Matt, let us out of here! Killing your family isn't the only way to save them from Warrington Chase!"

"It is," he replies. "You don't know what it's been like. Ever since we moved in, this *thing* has been testing us, teasing us at the edge of our minds. It's possessed all of us at one point or another. I heard both my children say the most awful things, things that they shouldn't even understand. I can't let them become corrupted like this, but I can't get us out of here, so this is the only way. At least none of us will have to suffer now."

"Try the window!" I shout, turning to Diane. She seems frozen in place, so after a moment I push her toward the window at the other end of the room. "Try it! We have to get out of here!"

When she still fails to respond, I hurry to the window and pull it open. When I lean out, I quickly find that my memory has been serving me well: the window looks out onto the roof of the garden shed, which means that anyone should be able to climb out fairly easily and run to safety.

"Hurry!" I yell, waving at the two children,

gesturing for them to join me. "There's a way out but you have to be quick!"

They race toward me, and I help first Katie and then Lance out through the window. They clamber onto the roof of the shed, coughing wildly, and then they crawl to the far end.

"You can jump down from there," I tell them, as Diane joins me at the window and we both look out. "The neighbors have to see the flames soon. Go and tell them to call for help."

"I can't leave Matt behind," Diane says, and I turn to see that there's a determined expression in her eyes. "He's my husband," she adds with a hint of desperation. "I know he's not really himself right now, but I have to help him."

"I can help Matt," I tell her. "You need to help your children right now."

We both turn and see the children on the far end of the shed's roof. They're both trying to find a way down, but they seem hesitant to jump and I'm worried they might hurt themselves. A moment later Diane clambers past me, climbing out onto the roof before turning to me again.

"Are you coming?" she asks.

"I think there's still time to save Matt," I reply. "Get Lance and Katie away from here, and call the fire brigade. I'm going to see if I can talk some sense into Matt and get him to leave."

"But if -"

"Go!" I add, pushing her away from the window before turning and looking back across the room. "Don't worry, I think I know how to help him."

***

Once I've forced the door open, I keep my shirt over the bottom half of my face as I stumble out onto the landing. The heat is intense, almost forcing me back, and when I look down the stairs I immediately see that the flames are far too strong. I want to find some way to get to Matt, but already my promises are ringing hollow in the back of my mind and I'm worried that I'll just have to follow Diane and the children out onto the roof of the shed.

"Matt?" I call out, hoping against hope that he might be able to hear me. "I'm here!"

I wait, but there's no reply. A moment later I hear an ominous creaking sound coming from the floor beneath me, and I realize that this entire house is in danger of collapsing.

"I'm sorry," I add, turning to head back into the bedroom, "if -"

Suddenly I'm grabbed from behind and pulled back, and a moment later Matt spins me around and slams me hard against the wall. Before I have a chance to react, he presses an arm against my throat and pushes firmly, pinning me in place as he leans closer. As I look into his eyes, however, I quickly realize that he has the same expression I saw on Diane's face back in the chapel, which can only mean one thing.

"Warrington Chase," I whisper.

"Perhaps I was greedy," he sneers. "Perhaps I should never have tried to talk all four of them. Perhaps just this one will do."

"You can't just take someone's body!" I shout, as the heat from the fire becomes even more intense. "These people are a family!"

"I can take what I want," he tells me. "They all tried to fight back, but they were too weak. All I ever wanted was the chance to cheat death. Is that really too much to ask?"

"You can't do it at the expense of innocent people!" I snap back at him angrily.

"There's no such thing as innocence," he replies. "Believe me, when you've been in the minds of these idiots the way I have, you quickly learn that everyone has some kind of weakness."

I try to push him away, but he's far too strong. As he in turn pushes me against the wall, I hear another loud splitting sound and I look down just in time to see that the floorboards are starting to crack. The fire was started downstairs, but now the inferno is reaching up to swallow the top floor as well and I know we only have a matter of seconds before the entire house collapses.

"Dad!" Lance yells from outside. "Where are you?"

"Daddy!" Katie screams. "Daddy, come out!"

"Do you hear that?" I ask, looking into Matt's eyes and hoping against hope to spot some hint of his real mind. "Your children want you, Matt. Killing them wouldn't have saved them. I know this must feel hopeless now, but if we can get out of here I'll find a way to help you. Warrington Chase can't possess all four of you at once and -"

"He's trying!" Matt replies, although I know this is still Chase speaking through his voice. "Oh, how he's trying, but he can't take back control."

"You can, Matt," I continue, before starting to cough as thicker and thicker smoke fills the landing. "Listen to them, Matt. Your children need you!"

"Daddy!"

"They're terrified," I add, still watching his eyes for some hint of a breakthrough. "Do you really want this to be their final memory of you? Do you really want them to remember the night you tried to kill them? Are you sure you can't find some way to break his hold over you?"

I wait for an answer, but now his face has fallen still. He's still pressing me hard against the wall, and I'm still desperately hoping that Jessica might once again come to the rescue, but after a few seconds I start to wonder whether I might at last have managed to get through to the real Matt. I open my mouth to ask whether he can hear me, but at the last second I realize that I might accidentally distract him. Instead I continue to wait, still praying that somehow he might have been strong enough.

And then, slowly, he starts laughing.

"Matt -"

"I'll just take another of them," he sneers. "There are three of them out there, and I can slip into one of their bodies easily enough. There's really nothing you can do to stop me."

Reaching into my pocket, I try to find my phone, but instead my fingers quickly feel the edges of the crucifix. I hesitate for a moment, and then I pull it out and hold it up, hoping that perhaps the mere sight of this thing might be enough to drive an evil spirit away.

Instead, his laugh only grows.

"Is that supposed to scare me?" he chuckles. "Do you really think no-one's ever tried that before?"

"Fine," I reply, adjusting my grip on the crucifix, "then how about we try this instead?"

Without giving him a chance to react, I turn the crucifix around and stab it into his left eye. He lets out a pained cry and pulls back, but he quickly grabs my arm and pulls me closer again. I can already see blood running from his injured eye, and after a moment he looks at me with his remaining eye and I see the real Matt Hooper again.

"Run!" he gasps. "The pain's making me stronger, but you have to run!"

"Not without you!" I tell him.

"I can take him to Hell with me," he sneers. "That's where he belongs, but you have to hurry because this whole place is about to go down. Just tell Diane and the kids that I love them, and that I'm only doing this because it's the only way I can be sure they'll be safe forever. If I die with him still inside me like this, it's going to take him a very long time to come back. If he ever does."

I hesitate, still convinced that there must be some other way, but a moment later part of the ceiling collapses, almost crushing us both.

"Run!" Matt shouts, stepping back as thick smoke almost entirely obscures him from my view. "Tell them!"

At that moment the rest of the ceiling comes crashing down. I step forward and try to find Matt, but the flames quickly beat me back and finally I turn and back into the bedroom. I clamber out of the window and throw myself onto the roof of the shed, and then I crawl on all fours to the edge and drop down, landing hard on the grass. I let out a pained gasp as I roll onto my back, and as I look back up at the house I see the entire roof collapsing as the building falls in on itself in an enormous inferno.

CHAPTER TWENTY-EIGHT

"WHERE IS HE?" DIANE gasps as I scramble across the lawn, trying to get to safety. "Where's Matt?"

"I couldn't -"

Before I can get another word out, I break into a huge coughing fit. Leaning forward, I struggle to even breathe as I desperately try to clear my throat. Looking at my hands, I see that they're partially burned thanks to the flames in the house, and then I turn just as another ear-splitting crashing sound signals the building's final collapse. What was left of number three Davis Drive tumbles to the ground, and I'm almost blinded by the intensity of the flames.

"I couldn't get him out," I stammer, as I realize that there's no point watching the fire and hoping for a miracle. "I tried, but he said it was the only way to keep you all safe. He was -"

Suddenly another part of the house collapses. I thought it was done, but evidently a section of the wall had somehow still been standing. As a wall of heat hits me, I scramble to my feet and take a couple of steps back, and a moment later I hear Diane sobbing as she tries to console her children. In the distance, the sirens of fire engines can already be heard getting closer.

"I'm so sorry," I tell Diane, not really knowing what else to say. "I tried to get him out but..."

My voice trails off, and I know that there's no way I can make any of this better. After a moment, however, I realize that both children are really weeping, and that Diane's sobbing as well, which means – as far as I can tell that – Warrington Chase is no longer possessing any of them. I turn and look back at the flames; Matt's body is in there somewhere, and I'm starting to think that his plan might have worked. Chase was possessing him, or at least trying to, at the moment of his death, which means that Chase is now in the same place as Matt. I can only hope that the rest of his plan will work too, and that Chase never again finds a way back to the world of the living.

"It's okay," Diane says, hugging her children tight. "Just try not to cry, okay?"

"Is Daddy coming back?" Katie asks.

"Daddy did a very brave thing," she replies, before looking up at me with fearful, tear-filled eyes. "That's right, isn't it?" she continues. "Matt saved us."

"He did," I tell her, and now I can hear fire engines pulling to a screeching halt nearby, and voices yelling instructions at one another. "He did the only thing he could think of, to save you from that monster. And he wanted me to tell you how much he loved you."

"Don't cry," Diane says, ignoring me as she continues to try to comfort Katie and Lance. "Please, try not to cry. Daddy's at peace now."

***

A few hours later, as the first rays of morning light spread across the village, fire engines and police cars are still parked all around on Davis Drive. Number three is nothing more now than a pile of rubble, and neighbors from all along the road are watching from the police cordon at the far junction.

"Fancy seeing you here."

Sitting on the grassy slope at the rear of the back fence, I look up and see that Detective Reid is making his way over. I knew he'd be on his way, but I suppose deep down I was hoping that I might get the all-clear to leave before having to talk to him.

"I've talked to Diane Hooper," he tells me as he stops a few feet away. "Obviously this isn't my case, but I wanted to come along and see if I might be able to help with anything. According to Diane, her husband had been struggling with his mental health for a while. She thinks that in the end he simply snapped."

"She said that?" I reply, although I suppose I shouldn't be shocked that Diane chose not to mention all the stuff with the ghostly figures. "I mean... that sounds about right."

"The part I don't get, though," he continues, "is how you ended up here."

"I told the other office, I -"

"You said you were just walking past and you raced in to help when you saw the flames. I read his notes." He pauses, and I can tell that he's extremely skeptical. "So you were walking past in the middle of the night, huh?"

"I was trying to clear my head."

"Your hands look painful."

"It's just some superficial burns," I tell him, holding my hands up so that he can see the red marks. "The paramedic says I'll be fine."

"And is there anything else you think you should tell me, Ms. Willow?" he asks.

"Like what?"

"I don't know, but I thought you might have a few ideas. Is there anything else that happened during the night that you think might be relevant." He glances over his shoulder for a moment before turning to me again. "Because I've got to be honest, I don't think Diane gave us the whole story."

"You don't?"

"She's a grieving widow, so no-one wants to push her too hard. And Curtis, the guy who's handling the case, seems satisfied. But I've got this kind of sixth sense that helps me figure out when something's wrong, and right now that sixth sense is tingling. If you know anything, Ms. Willow, I'd really love you to share your thoughts with me."

"I don't know anything," I tell him as I get to my feet. "Am I free to go?"

"As far as I know. It's not my case, remember. We know where you live if we need to ask any follow-up questions. You're not planning on leaving town soon, are you?"

"Am I not allowed to?" I ask.

"I didn't say that," he replies with a calm smile that's clearly calculated to put me at ease. "There's no need to get jumpy, Ms. Willow. You're not getting paranoid, are you?"

"I'm sorry, I'm just tired," I tell him. "Are Diane and the children going to be okay?"

"Some relatives are on their way. I'm not sure how long it takes a woman to feel okay after her husband kills himself and almost takes the rest of the family with him, but I'm sure she'll be in safe hands. Meanwhile, we're still trying to find a motive beyond the simple suggestion that Matt Hooper lost his mind. Did he do or say anything that you think could give us any insight?"

"How could he have done?" I lie. "I didn't really get to speak to him tonight."

"Oh, that's right," he replies, even though he was clearly trying to trick me. "I'm sorry, I must have been getting a little confused. You know what it's like when you're up all night and you're running around getting up to all sorts of things, and you just don't manage to keep track of everything." He pauses again, and this time I feel certain that he's really studying me as he keeps his gaze fixed firmly on my eyes. "You're very much free to go, Ms. Willow," he adds. "I can even arrange for someone to drive you home, if you'd like."

"No, thank you," I say, stepping past him and making my way toward the street. I feel as if I'm on the verge of collapse, but there's no way I'm taking an offer of help from this guy. Not until I know exactly what he wants.

As I walk away, I fully expect him to call out to me with 'one last thing', but he says nothing. Instead, I make my way past the fire engines and I can't help but feel Reid's gaze burning into the back of my head. I tell myself that I mustn't turn and look, but finally I do just that, and to my surprise I find that he's nowhere to be seen; I look all around, but I guess even a guy like Reid has to get on with the job eventually. He definitely has his suspicions about me, however, and to be honest I'm not even sure that I can blame him. From his perspective, I must certainly seem like something of a mystery.

"Hey, do you know what happened?"

Turning, I see that a woman is watching me from behind the police cordon, her eyes wide like saucers in expectation of some gossip. Several other people are huddled nearby, also waiting for me to say something.

"I heard some guy went mad and tried to kill his family," the woman continues eagerly. "Do you know if that's true?"

"No," I reply, shaking my head slightly, "that's not true at all."

"It's not?"

She seems genuinely disappointed.

"He was trying to save them," I add. "He *did* save them. I just wish he could have found another way."

"Oh," she says as I duck under the cordon and head past the group. "Well, that's a bit... Okay, I suppose..."

As I walk away, I can't help but think that this woman and her friends would have much preferred to hear that Matt Hooper completely lost his mind and tried to butcher his wife and children. That, at least, would have given them some real meat to chew off the bone. Part of me wants to turn back and fill them in on exactly what happened, but I guess there's no real point, and then – as I reach the end of the street – I stop and look back at the ruins of the house. In that moment, I realize that there might still be one thing I can do to help.

***

A few minutes later, having made my way around to the rear of the property, I look down at the rotten stump of wood poking out of the grass. This is all that remains of the old gallows, and as I reach up and touch the side of my neck I remember the sensation of the hatch dropping and the noose tightening around my neck.

I kick at the stump several times, and to my surprise it breaks away fairly easily, until soon there's nothing left except a few flaked splinters strewn across the damp grass.

CHAPTER TWENTY-NINE

HUNDREDS OF YEARS EARLIER, Warrington Chase stood on the village green and slowly turned to look around at the various higgeldy-piggledy buildings of Candleward. Every few seconds someone emerged from one of the buildings, setting off on some chore as part of their daily life, getting on with the mundane activities that kept village life running.

"Idiots," Chase murmured under his breath. "Pathetic, pointless fools."

Nearby, a man called out, and Chase turned to see a particularly scruffy-looking fellow herding some sheep across the green's far end. Several people kept animals on the open green space, and the cacophonous noise of sheep and goats and chickens at least made the center of the village feel constantly alive and constantly busy. Chase saw that the place was at least managing to survive, although – having arrived several months earlier – he still felt nothing but contempt for the tiny little lives of so many unimportant morons.

"Living in squalor and dirt," he continued. "You lack even the notion of a better life. Of ambition. And that is why your lives will ultimately be completely forgotten."

***

Later, as he sat at his desk in the small cottage he rented near the green, Chase looked down at his notes and tried to spot some logic in all the chaos.

"It's here," he whispered, as a candle flickered nearby on the desk. "I know it's all here, all the secrets are so close, I just need to find a way to access them."

He turned to another page of notes, then another, convinced that at any moment he was about to make a breakthrough. As the minutes passed, however, he felt his frustration grow until finally – with a sense of exasperation – he leaned back in his creaking chair and looked out the window.

A woman was making her way past the cottage, carrying a heavy-looking bag.

"It must be so easy to be simple," Chase murmured, watching her with great interest. "To not think of the grander matters of existence. Sometimes I wish I had not been born with such a curious mind, yet..."

His voice trailed off as he tried to empty his mind of all cares and concerns, to limit his thoughts so that all he heard in his head might be silence. This, he sometimes felt, might be how to truly draw out the wonders of creation; he told himself that if he could cease all earthly thoughts, he might yet be able to determine the true nature of reality. Yet as the second passed, and as the woman shuffled out of sight, Chase realized that he had made no progress whatsoever, and he began to wonder whether he might yet need some major shift of his strategy.

"I've reached the limits of this life," he reminded himself, keeping his voice low in the hush of the afternoon light. "There must be more. There must be something out there, some means by which I can extend my existence and understand everything there is to understand."

Feeling increasingly weary, he hauled himself up and stepped away from the desk. Light rain was starting to fall against the windowpanes, and in that moment he realized that his tired old bones were starting to ache. He held up his left hand, clenching and unclenching his fist in the process, and he saw that his skin bore the marks of age. He remembered having seen his own father's hand, and his father's father, and he knew that he was approaching the time when he'd have to join them in death.

"I refuse," he said softly, clenching his fist once more. "There is a way to defeat even death itself."

**

By the time he'd left the cottage and was making his way along one of the village's narrow streets, more and more rain was falling. Lacking a proper coat for the weather, he hurried past puddles and tried to stay as close as possible to the walls, keen to remain as dry as possible.

Reaching the bottom of the hill, he saw the public house nearby and then he looked out across the village green. A gaggle of geese made their way past, honking loudly, and a moment later a woman hurried the other way, chasing the birds back toward some other part of the green. Chase stopped for a moment and considered the utter inevitability of the woman's defeat; the geese would never listen to her properly, not permanently, and he marveled at the ability of humans to dedicate their lives to tasks of such utter unimportance.

How could they accept the inevitability of death?

"Afternoon, Mr. Chase," one of the locals said as he made his way past, heading up the hill.

"You won't want to be out for too long, not in this weather. The wind's blowing from the south and that always means the rain's going to get worse before it gets better."

"I don't need your advice," Chase replied. "You'd do well to mind your own business."

"Just a fair warning," the man continued, struggling a little with his hip as he walked away. "No need to bite my head off."

Annoyed by the man's interference, Chase took a step forward, only to stop immediately as he found himself suddenly very breathless. He leaned against the wall, telling himself that this was merely a brief interlude of ill health, but if anything the sensation began to grow. Leaning back, he took a series of big, deep breaths as he tried to fill his lungs, yet at the same time he could already feel his body starting to fail. These health scares had been coming and going for a while now, pushing him to work harder and harder on his research, but now he felt for the first time that his weak and tiring body was actually holding him back.

"I've been a fool," he whispered, as he felt his body becoming as heavy as lead. "I've been searching for the answers in books and notes, when truly they're out here somewhere in the natural world. It just takes a visionary such as myself to see them."

He forced himself to start walking again,

skirting the edge of the village green as he set out to finally uncover the true secret of life after death.

***

"I never usually come out this far," Joseph Fetterman said as he led his cousin Nathaniel through the forest. "There's not much here except a few flowers, and I don't see much point in looking at those."

"We could pick a few and give them to girls in the village," Nathaniel suggested.

"Any girl in particular?" Joseph asked, glancing at him with a smile.

"There are a few I've got in mind," Nathaniel admitted, somewhat shyly. "I want to keep my options open for a little while yet, though. I wouldn't -"

"Stop!" Joseph said suddenly, reaching out with a hand to keep him from going any further.

Before he had a chance to ask what was wrong, Nathaniel saw the body of an elderly man resting on the ground, in a clearing between several trees.

"Who is it?" he asked.

"I've seen him in the village," Joseph told him. "I can't remember his name, but by all accounts he's neither a popular nor a very eminent gentleman. In fact, I've always been warned to keep away from him. There are some who say he dabbles in arts that any good man should leave alone."

"Such as?"

"I don't want to even say the words out loud," Joseph continued, "but we should head back home and let someone know that we've found him." He paused, but even from a distance he could see the old man's glassy dead eyes staring up toward the sky. "Someone'll know what to do with him. It doesn't look like there's been any foul play, only that he upped and died. That happens sometimes."

"But who was he?" Nathaniel asked. "I mean, who was he *really*?"

Joseph paused for a moment as he stared at the body. Considering the question, he thought of the few times he'd spotted the strange man in the village.

"No-one," he said finally.

"No-one?"

"No-one." He shrugged. "Just like most people are no-one. They live and they die, and that's it. He'll be buried, and after a few years I don't suppose anyone'll ever remember that he ever even existed. You've got to accept, that's just how the worlds works. There's not anyone who can fight against that."

As they turned and walked away, they left the body of Warrington Chase in the grass. A cool breeze blew across the clearing, disturbing the strands of hair that had fallen across the dead man's face; his motionless eyes stared out, reflecting the cool gray sky, even as – somewhere else entirely – his soul already plotted its return.

CHAPTER THIRTY

Today...

"WARRINGTON CHASE," FARRAR SAYS as we stand in his little study at Torfork Tower. "I fear that everything I thought I knew about that man is wrong. Even the time period in which he lived, unless..."

He pauses, staring down at his notes, before finally turning to me. His eyes are watery; not, I'm fairly sure, because of tears, but because of tiredness. He has the hangdog expression of someone who hasn't slept much lately, and I'm fairly sure that he's been extremely busy while I was away dealing with everything that happened at Davis Drive. I've filled him in on the basics, but I still can't help wishing that he'd been at the house with me; he might have figured out a way to save the entire family without losing Matt.

"What if he *did* manage to come back?" he continues. "After he died, and before today? I'm sure the details you uncovered don't match up with the date of the institute's foundation. Thank you, Mercy, you've given me a great deal to think about, although I have to admit that I'm a little overawed by it all. I think I might have to start my research all over again, right from the beginning."

"Do you think he's really gone this time?" I ask.

"With a man like Chase, you can never be sure," he replies. "However, I can't imagine that he'll be able to claw his way back in the near future. If he *does* return, I suspect it will be long after both you and I have shuffled off this mortal coil. And then he'll be somebody else's problem to deal with."

"I still don't quite understand why he picked that particular house," I tell him. "There are other loose ends, too. I saw the ghost of a woman, but I have no idea who she was."

"Not all mysteries can be solved."

"And I'm not convinced that it was always Radcliffe in that cupboard. At least one time, I think it might have been some other force."

"You might be right."

"I don't understand half of this!"

"And perhaps you never will. I suppose he

had to pick someone to focus on, some poor family to try to control. It's just a good job that Mr. Radcliffe's ghost was still around to try to slow him down. For all his faults, this Radcliffe fellow seems to have been a well-meaning, if perhaps slightly misguided at times, man of the law."

"I could use a quiet week," I mutter, as I pick up some of the other papers and sift through them. "How do you keep track of it all? This whole situation feels like a complete mess."

"That's why I have to focus," he replies with a faint, sad smile. "Every time I think I'm close to a resolution, I simply uncover more questions. Right now, I fear that I'm back at the start." He pauses, and I can't help but notice that he's standing a little strangely, as if he's once again feeling some kind of pain in his belly. "That's the worst part," he mutters. "I'm an old man and I don't have much time left. What little time I *do* have, I can't afford to waste."

"Can I help?"

"I think I just need to be left alone," he says, before taking a moment to clear his throat. He still seems ill, but I don't know how to seriously broach the subject; every time I've tried before, he's either brushed my concerns off or become a little hostile. "I shall perhaps pop down to the pub for one of their pies, however. Would you like to meet there around, say, six o'clock?"

After making plans with Farrar, I'm left

feeling somewhat directionless as I walk back through the village. Technically today is supposed to be my day off from work, and Horace tends to disapprove of me working when I should be taking a break, but I'm starting to think that I should perhaps just grab some paperwork and get on with things at home. On the way to the office, however, I wander toward Davis Drive and I see the cordoned-off site where number three used to stand. I should head away, but I still feel as if there are answers hiding just out of sight.

And then, as I head around the rear of the line of houses, I find myself looking down once more at the spot where the wooden stump used to stand.

"He's still here," a voice says suddenly.

Turning, I'm shocked to see that Diane Hooper is watching me from nearby.

"The kids are with my mum," she adds, stepping toward me. "I think they need time to deal with the loss of their father. Katie keeps asking if he's coming back. I think she knows deep down that he isn't, but somehow she's clinging to the hope. I don't really blame her."

She stops and looks toward the wreckage of the house.

"He's still here," she says again. "I don't know how I know, I can just feel Matt's presence. I had a dream about him the other night."

"That must have been comforting," I reply, although I know those words probably aren't very helpful.

"He came to me while I was asleep," she continues, "and told me that everything's going to be okay. He told me that he can keep that Chase guy away from us forever now. He told me that I have to move on with my life, but that he'll always be keeping us safe. Does that sound crazy?"

"Not at all," I tell her.

"He also told me to forget about the house," she adds. "He wants me to deal with the lawyers and make sure that after the rubble's been cleared away, no-one builds here again. I suppose that should be easy enough, since we still own the land. It'll be a big financial hit, we'll have to live with my mum for a long time, but Matt was really insistent. He said that we should leave the place empty, just in case he loses his grip on Chase." She pauses, and I can see the uncertainty in her eyes. "Do you think it's true?" she asks. "All of it. Do you think it really happened, or am I just losing my mind?"

"I think we don't have the whole story," I reply diplomatically. "We've seen snatches of something happening, something that was much bigger than any of us. We dealt with the part we could see, with the part that just about made sense to us, but I think something happened here that was bigger than any of us can comprehend. It's possible that the human mind just can't deal with certain realities."

"How do I explain that to my children?" she asks. "They've lost their father."

As we walk back into the village so she can get to her car, Diane and I talk some more about Matt's final moments. She's still trying to make sense of it all, and I completely understand that impulse, but I'm starting to think that Farrar was right: there are forces working beyond our line of sight, powerful forces that don't obey our laws, and there's really no way we can ever truly understand what we're facing. Not without losing our minds, at least. When faced with these things, humans seem pretty flimsy.

Once Diane has driven away, I head to the office and grab some paperwork. Horace isn't around, but I find some notes that he's left behind, one relating to the old Candleward lighthouse and one asking me to – again – call Frank Chipson and talk to him about Gower Grange. I have no idea why the Chipsons are still bothering me, but I'm starting to think that I should just grab the bull by the horns and go out there to talk to him. After all, he seems remarkably persistent and I really don't think that ignoring him is going to be a successful strategy.

On my way home, I stop by the library, figuring that I might as well get some research done. The place closes soon, but I can fit in an hour of work so I head straight into the research room. As soon as I open the door, however, I see Mr. Allan sitting at one of the computers, and he immediately gets to his feet as soon as he spots me.

"Hi," I say, forcing a smile, "I think -"

"I'm so glad you're here," he replies, and I'm struck by the sense of fear and desperation in his voice. "Ms. Willow, you know rather a lot about ghosts, do you not?"

"Well... I think so," I say cautiously, "but -"

"I've finally finished my research," he continues, interrupting me, "and I don't think I can ignore the truth for a moment longer." He steps closer. "I need your help. I'm begging you, can't you at least take a look and see whether you can help?"

"What exactly's going on?" I ask.

"It's a ghost," he stammers, and I can tell now that his panic is genuine. "My home is haunted, Ms. Willow, and I can't stand it anymore. Please, you have to help me!"

AMY CROSS

EPILOGUE

Twenty years earlier...

"I'M SICK AND TIRED of this nonsense," Evans says with a heavy sigh as he slams his keys on the table and turns to storm out of the room. "If I have to clean up one more mess left by some incompetent moron, I swear I'll start bashing some heads together!"

Sitting completely still in the day-room, I continue to stare out the window until I hear his footsteps disappearing toward the far end of the service corridor. I can feel my heart pounding, and deep down I know that this is the moment I've been waiting for; over the past few weeks I've been plotting and planning, trying to work out exactly how and when to break free from this hospital. I know that I've earned some degree of trust, and I also know that I won't get a second chance. I listen as a door slams in the distance, and I now know that I don't have time to hesitate.

I'm scared, but I have to move.

"Come on, Jessica," I whisper as I get to my feet and hurry to the nurses' station, quickly scooping up the keys and then making my way to one of the other doors. "This is precisely when I need your... skills."

As soon as I'm through the door, I know that I've gone past the point of no return. Based on all my previous observations, I figure I've got maybe three minutes to reach the loading bay and then another two minutes to reach the fence at the far end of the yard. Once I've scaled that fence and I'm on the other side, my next task will be to disappear into the darkness surrounding the forest; that's the part that I haven't really been able to plan for, although based on a few snippets of overheard conversations I *think* there's a river somewhere nearby.

"Move," I remind myself, as I set off again along the corridor. "You've literally only got seconds to spare."

Once I'm through the next door, I find myself in the boiler room. So far, my plan's going exactly as expected, although a moment later I take a step forward and suddenly feel something tugging me back. I look around; there's no sign of anyone, but I can already feel Jessica twisting her way up through my chest and preparing to take over.

"Finally," I say with a sigh. "Where have you been?"

"Where's Annabelle?" she asks, her voice echoing through our shared mind.

"Sleeping," I explain. "I told you, I've found a way to make her settle. Now we just have to get out of here."

I take a step toward the door, only to feel myself getting held back again.

"Not so fast," Jessica says firmly. "I'm all for getting out of here, but first that asshole Evans has to pay for everything he's done to us. Not to mention Doctor Ross, who seriously needs to be taught a few manners."

"That's not part of the plan," I remind her.

"I'm changing the plan."

She tries to force us to turn. I reach out and almost touch a scalding hot pipe running along the wall. Stopping myself, I realize that Jessica means business and that she's going to jeopardize everything we've been working toward. I should have known that she was going to try to take over, but I can't let her do that. She gets too emotional, and although I hate Evans with every ounce of my being, the last thing I want is for us to end up with more blood on our hands. Even now I can feel her trying to take control, although I quickly manage to push her back down.

"Not now," I say firmly. "You focus on keeping Annabelle contained, and I'll focus on getting us as far away from this hospital as possible. Deal?"

I wait, but a moment later I hear voices in the distance, yelling at one another in panic.

A moment later I realize I can already feel Jessica starting to stir again. She's rippling up through my – *our* – body, and she's making a point of wriggling against our spine. She's not quite ready to strike back, but she wants me to remember that she's here. As I hear footsteps racing through the hospital, I know I don't have long before I'm caught, so I have to quickly find some way to end this madness once and for all.

Turning, I look over at the metal pipe that runs up the far wall. I already know that the pipe is burning hot, and I'm starting to come up with a plan. I just don't know that I'm brave enough to go through with something that's going to be so painful. At the same time, I'm starting to realize that I don't have any other choice.

"Coward," Jessica sneers, her voice filling my thoughts. "You don't have the guts."

"Oh no?" I reply. "Watch me."

"I always laugh when you try to be tough," she says as I step toward the pipe. I can already feel the heat radiating out toward me. "You're pathetic,

Mercy. You know that, right? There's no way you can ever be in charge of our existence, not really. You've served your purpose, and that's all well and good, but when things get serious we all know you need me to take the wheel."

I stop in front of the pipe.

"You're not a complete person," she says firmly.

"I -"

"You're a fantasy," she adds. "A mirage. You're a made-up identity. You're a do-gooder who can't possibly exist in the real world. You're like one side of one tiny percentage of an actual human being. Face it, Mercy, you're just not made for this life, so why are you trying to draw this pathetic drama out for so long?"

"I'm not letting you take back control," I tell her. "Last time -"

"I won't do all that stuff again," she insists. "You know it's better when I'm in charge, Mercy. I'll still let you out occasionally, when you're needed, but most of the time you can sleep safely in my thoughts. You were useful for a while, but now – for the most part – I'm done with you. So let's not have any more of this nonsense."

I stare at the pipe for a few more seconds, before turning away.

"That's right," Jessica chuckles, and now she sounds so smug. "See? I told you there wasn't going to be any drama today. Now just sit back and let me take -"

"Go to Hell."

Before she has a chance to reply, I step back and press my spine against the metal pipe. I immediately scream as I feel the hot metal burning into my skin, and I can hear Jessica shouting in the back of my mind and begging me to stop. I know I should pull away, but instead I press harder, willing the metal to burn all the way through to my spine if that's what it takes.

"Get out!" I scream. "Get out! Get out! Get out!"

BOOKS IN THIS SERIES

Also by Amy Cross

**The Haunting of Nelson Street
(The Ghosts of Crowford book 1)**

Crowford, a sleepy coastal town in the south of England,
might seem like an oasis of calm and tranquility.
Beneath the surface, however, dark secrets are waiting to
claim fresh victims, and ghostly figures plot revenge.

Having finally decided to leave the hustle of London,
Daisy and Richard Johnson buy two houses on Nelson
Street, a picturesque street in the center of Crowford.
One house is perfect and ready to move into, while the
other is a fire-ravaged wreck that needs a lot of work.
They figure they have plenty of time to work on the
damaged house while Daisy recovers from a traumatic
event.

Soon, they discover that the two houses share a common
link to the past. Something awful once happened on
Nelson Street, something that shook the town to its core.

Also by Amy Cross

The Revenge of the Mercy Belle
(The Ghosts of Crowford book 2)

The year is 1950, and a great tragedy has struck the town of Crowford. Three local men have been killed in a storm, after their fishing boat the Mercy Belle sank. A mysterious fourth man, however, was rescue. Nobody knows who he is, or what he was doing on the Mercy Belle... and the man has lost his memory.

Five years later, messages from the dead warn of impending doom for Crowford. The ghosts of the Mercy Belle's crew demand revenge, and the whole town is being punished. The fourth man still has no memory of his previous existence, but he's married now and living under the named Edward Smith. As Crowford's suffering continues, the locals begin to turn against him.

What really happened on the night the Mercy Belle sank? Did the fourth man cause the tragedy? And will Crowford survive if this man is not sent to meet his fate?

Also by Amy Cross

The Devil, the Witch and the Whore
(The Deal book 1)

"Leave the forest alone. Whatever's out there, just let it be. Don't make it angry."

When a horrific discovery is made at the edge of town, Sheriff James Kopperud realizes the answers he seeks might be waiting beyond in the vast forest. But everybody in the town of Deal knows that there's something out there in the forest, something that should never be disturbed. A deal was made long ago, a deal that was supposed to keep the town safe. And if he insists on investigating the murder of a local girl, James is going to have to break that deal and head out into the wilderness.

Meanwhile, James has no idea that his estranged daughter Ramsey has returned to town. Ramsey is running from something, and she thinks she can find safety in the vast tunnel system that runs beneath the forest. Before long, however, Ramsey finds herself coming face to face with creatures that hide in the shadows. One of these creatures is known as the devil, and another is known as the witch. They're both waiting for the whore to arrive, but for very different reasons. And soon Ramsey is offered a terrible deal, one that could save or destroy the entire town, and maybe even the world.

Also by Amy Cross

The Soul Auction

"I saw a woman on the beach. I watched her face a demon."

Thirty years after her mother's death, Alice Ashcroft is drawn back to the coastal English town of Curridge. Somebody in Curridge has been reviewing Alice's novels online, and in those reviews there have been tantalizing hints at a hidden truth. A truth that seems to be linked to her dead mother.

"Thirty years ago, there was a soul auction."

Once she reaches Curridge, Alice finds strange things happening all around her. Something attacks her car. A figure watches her on the beach at night. And when she tries to find the person who has been reviewing her books, she makes a horrific discovery.

What really happened to Alice's mother thirty years ago? Who was she talking to, just moments before dropping dead on the beach? What caused a huge rockfall that nearly tore a nearby cliff-face in half? And what sinister presence is lurking in the grounds of the local church?

Also by Amy Cross

Darper Danver: The Complete First Series

Five years ago, three friends went to a remote cabin in the woods and tried to contact the spirit of a long-dead soldier. They thought they could control whatever happened next. They were wrong...

Newly released from prison, Cassie Briggs returns to Fort Powell, determined to get her life back on track. Soon, however, she begins to suspect that an ancient evil still lurks in the nearby cabin. Was the mysterious Darper Danver really destroyed all those years ago, or does her spirit still linger, waiting for a chance to return?

As Cassie and her ex-boyfriend Fisher are finally forced to face the truth about what happened in the cabin, they realize that Darper isn't ready to let go of their lives just yet. Meanwhile, a vengeful woman plots revenge for her brother's murder, and a New York ghost writer arrives in town to uncover the truth. Before long, strange carvings begin to appear around town and blood starts to flow once again.

Also by Amy Cross

The Ghost of Molly Holt

"Molly Holt is dead. There's nothing to fear in this house."

When three teenagers set out to explore an abandoned house in the middle of a forest, they think they've found the location where the infamous Molly Holt video was filmed.

They've found much more than that...

Tim doesn't believe in ghosts, but he has a crush on a girl who does. That's why he ends up taking her out to the house, and it's also why he lets her take his only flashlight. But as they explore the house together, Tim and Becky start to realize that something else might be lurking in the shadows.

Something that, ten years ago, suffered unimaginable pain.

Something that won't rest until a terrible wrong has been put right.

Also by Amy Cross

American Coven

He kidnapped three women and held them in his basement. He thought they couldn't fight back. He was wrong...

Snatched from the street near her home, Holly Carter is taken to a rural house and thrown down into a stone basement. She meets two other women who have also been kidnapped, and soon Holly learns about the horrific rituals that take place in the house. Eventually, she's called upstairs to take her place in the ice bath.

As her nightmare continues, however, Holly learns about a mysterious power that exists in the basement, and which the three women might be able to harness. When they finally manage to get through the metal door, however, the women have no idea that their fight for freedom is going to stretch out for more than a decade, or that it will culminate in a final, devastating demonstration of their new-found powers.

Also by Amy Cross

The Ash House

Why would anyone ever return to a haunted house?

For Diane Mercer the answer is simple. She's dying of cancer, and she wants to know once and for all whether ghosts are real.

Heading home with her young son, Diane is determined to find out whether the stories are real. After all, everyone else claimed to see and hear strange things in the house over the years. Everyone except Diane had some kind of experience in the house, or in the little ash house in the yard.

As Diane explores the house where she grew up, however, her son is exploring the yard and the forest. And while his mother might be struggling to come to terms with her own impending death, Daniel Mercer is puzzled by fleeting appearances of a strange little girl who seems drawn to the ash house, and by strange, rasping coughs that he keeps hearing at night.

The Ash House is a horror novel about a woman who desperately wants to know what will happen to her when she dies, and about a boy who uncovers the shocking truth about a young girl's murder.

Also by Amy Cross

Haunted

Twenty years ago, the ghost of a dead little girl drove Sheriff Michael Blaine to his death.

Now, that same ghost is coming for his daughter.

Returning to the small town where she grew up, Alex Roberts is determined to live a normal, quiet life. For the residents of Railham, however, she's an unwelcome reminder of the town's darkest hour.

Twenty years ago, nine-year-old Mo Garvey was found brutally murdered in a nearby forest. Everyone thinks that Alex's father was responsible, but if the killer was brought to justice, why is the ghost of Mo Garvey still after revenge?

And how far will the real killer go to protect his secret, when Alex starts getting closer to the truth?

Haunted is a horror novel about a woman who has to face her past, about a town that would rather forget, and about a little girl who refuses to let death stand in her way.

AMY CROSS

Also by Amy Cross

The Curse of Wetherley House

"If you walk through that door, Evil Mary will get you."

When she agrees to visit a supposedly haunted house with an old friend, Rosie assumes she'll encounter nothing more scary than a few creaks and bumps in the night. Even the legend of Evil Mary doesn't put her off. After all, she knows ghosts aren't real. But when Mary makes her first appearance, Rosie realizes she might already be trapped.

For more than a century, Wetherley House has been cursed. A horrific encounter on a remote road in the late 1800's has already caused a chain of misery and pain for all those who live at the house. Wetherley House was abandoned long ago, after a terrible discovery in the basement, something has remained undetected within its room. And even the local children know that Evil Mary waits in the house for anyone foolish enough to walk through the front door.

Before long, Rosie realizes that her entire life has been defined by the spirit of a woman who died in agony. Can she become the first person to escape Evil Mary, or will she fall victim to the same fate as the house's other occupants?

AMY CROSS

Also by Amy Cross

The Ghosts of Hexley Airport

Ten years ago, more than two hundred people died in a horrific plane crash at Hexley Airport.

Today, some say their ghosts still haunt the terminal building.

When she starts her new job at the airport, working a night shift as part of the security team, Casey assumes the stories about the place can't be true. Even when she has a strange encounter in a deserted part of the departure hall, she's certain that ghosts aren't real.

Soon, however, she's forced to face the truth. Not only is there something haunting the airport's buildings and tarmac, but a sinister force is working behind the scenes to replicate the circumstances of the original accident. And as a snowstorm moves in, Hexley Airport looks set to witness yet another disaster.

AMY CROSS

Also by Amy Cross

The Girl Who Never Came Back

Twenty years ago, Charlotte Abernathy vanished while playing near her family's house. Despite a frantic search, no trace of her was found until a year later, when the little girl turned up on the doorstep with no memory of where she'd been.

Today, Charlotte has put her mysterious ordeal behind her, even though she's never learned where she was during that missing year. However, when her eight-year-old niece vanishes in similar circumstances, a fully-grown Charlotte is forced to make a fresh attempt to uncover the truth.

Originally published in 2013, the fully revised and updated version of *The Girl Who Never Came Back* tells the harrowing story of a woman who thought she could forget her past, and of a little girl caught in the tangled web of a dark family secret.

AMY CROSS

Also by Amy Cross

Asylum
(The Asylum Trilogy book 1)

"No-one ever leaves Lakehurst. The staff, the patients, the ghosts... Once you're here, you're stuck forever."

After shooting her little brother dead, Annie Radford is sent to Lakehurst psychiatric hospital for assessment. Hearing voices in her head, Annie is forced to undergo experimental new treatments devised by a mysterious old man who lives in the hospital's attic. It soon becomes clear that the hospital's staff, led by the vicious Nurse Winter, are hiding something horrific at Lakehurst.

As Annie struggles to survive the hospital, she learns more about Nurse Winter's own story. Once a promising young medical student, Kirsten Winter also heard voices in her head. Voices that traveled a long way to reach her. Voices that have a plan of their own. Voices that will stop at nothing to get what they want.

What kind of signals are being transmitted from the basement of the hospital? Who is the old man in the attic? Why are living human brains kept in jars? And what is the dark secret that lurks at the heart of the hospital?

AMY CROSS

BOOKS BY AMY CROSS

AMY CROSS

For more information, visit:

www.blackwychbooks.com

AMY CROSS

Printed in Great Britain
by Amazon